ONCE UPON A ROOMMATE

GREENMOUNT GIANTS #1

COPYRIGHT

No part of this publication may be reproduced, distributed, or transmitted in any form or by any means, including photocopying, recording, or other electronic or mechanical methods, without the prior written permission of the publisher.

This is a work of fiction. Any resemblance of characters to actual persons, living or dead, is purely coincidental. RUBY KNIGHT holds exclusive rights to this work.

Unauthorized duplication is prohibited.

Copyright © 2023 by RUBY KNIGHT

A NOTE FROM THE AUTHOR

Thank you so much for picking up a copy of

ONCE UPON A ROOMMATE

I hope you enjoy the beginning of Jett and Mila's story.

Come join us in Ruby Knight's Dark Romancers

DEDICATION

For my wild, uncontrollable and thoroughly unapologetic baby sister.

May you fly high with the angels.

It's not goodbye. It's see you later...

ONCE UPON A ROOMMATE

GREENMOUNT

GIANTS #1

CHAPTER ONE
JETT

I shouldn't be doing this.

I told myself I'd put a stop to my selfish and reckless behavior, yet here I am, balls deep inside another random puck bunny purely to pass away the time. Just another desperate chick in a long line of many who can't seem to stay away from me.

I can't complain.

Not really. Not when there are guys out there, guys who would kill to have the smallest taste, a little sample of what I have on tap. A never-ending, constant supply of pussy.

I'm grateful, for sure... but sometimes; times like tonight it can start to feel like a chore. Like some kind of service I'm obliged to offer. I should be happy. Fucking ecstatic because this is just another glorious perk which comes with the territory.

The territory of being the hottest jock Greenmount has ever seen, and by far the best.

I'm used to the attention.

I relish in the glory, in its golden glow and heated flames. I thrive from the unstoppable power as it feeds my body, fueling me, making me desperate for another hit—like an addict clucking, helplessly searching for my next fix.

I'm usually more than happy to put on the mother of all shows while enjoying the ride. I love nothing more than making sure these desperate groupies feel special...

Wanted...

Needed, even. But for one night only. For one glorious bittersweet night I give them complete access to all things me and Jett Junior. I'm a red-blooded male after all. I'm riddled with a never-ending inferno of raging hormones and endless amounts of testosterone to burn. I'm a guy with needs—lots of needs, so obviously I'm going to jump straight in, dick first.

It's my rite of passage to indulge. As hockey captain and golden boy of this town it's my job to ensure each and every one of them has a wild night to remember... and they do, but then they have to go and kill the mood and ruin it for themselves by catching feelings.

Feelings which will never be reciprocated.

It might sound bigheaded, obnoxious even, but this is nothing more than fact. Nothing but the truth of my reality. I'm yet to meet a chick who hasn't ended up growing some kind of unhealthy attachment to me or my dick, and it doesn't matter how many times I try to warn them, how hard I lay down my rules, they still fall hard and fast.

I like to make sure no one goes in blind. I let them know I'm down for a little fun, but so long as it's fun with zero strings. That's how it has to be and they'll take it, seal the deal without really thinking about it. They look at me with wide, hungry eyes, pretending to understand—acting like my word is gospel; all too eager to get up close and personal with the elusive Jett Jameson: *Captain of the Greenmount Giants*. The hot jock with endless secrets and demons hidden behind his mesmerizing jade green eyes, but the second I slide my dick deep inside their warm, wet, welcoming pussies they quickly forget all of the above.

They get all caught up in the moment, lost inside their delinquent little minds, somehow convincing themselves that they're special. Different to every girl before them. Each and every one of them foolishly believe they hold the power to break the wicked spell.

These chicks think they can do the impossible. Tame the wicked beast before the final petal falls.

They're fucked up, stupid and downright delusional thinking they hold the power to save me before I'm doomed to a lifetime of emptiness and loneliness for all eternity.

It's hilarious.

Totally laughable that each and every one of them could be so naïve.

The only thing falling around here is my dick, slowly deflating like an aged balloon when they turn all possessive—all territorial, desperately trying to sink their razor-sharp claws into something they can never have...

... that something being me.

I can kind of understand their reaction to some extent. These chicks, they're all quick to forget who I am while they're still high from taking a wild and unforgettable ride on my dick, but as soon as the moment is over—when I've had my use of them, they quickly come back down to earth with an almighty bang and as their minds begin to clear, when the pheromone induced haze starts to fade, they're reminded of exactly who I am.

I'm Jett Jameson.

I'm a motherfucking star.

I'm a heartless son of a bitch.

I'm a jock. Captain of the Giants.

I'm the king of Greenmount... the towns very own golden boy and that's how it will always stay.

Everyone loves me. It's no secret that guys want to be me, and the girls; they're fucking shameless. They'll do everything and anything they feel they need to do to be in with a shot of getting close to me. *To fuck me*. Again, this isn't me being bigheaded, it's the God's honest truth. The beautiful truth of my glorious reality.

I'm undefeated.

I'm indestructible...

And most important of all... I'm un-fucking-tamable.

There's not a single chick, a single pussy on this planet powerful enough to hold me and my dick captive. Not a fucking one. Sometimes I have to take a much-needed step back and remind myself that I didn't choose this life. This life chose me, and I plan to enjoy every beautiful second it has to offer.

Running a weary hand along my stubbled jaw, I tear myself away from my wayward thoughts and look down at the naked blonde splayed out beneath me, her smooth creamy flesh glistening in the moonlight as it seeps through my bedroom window, and I feel... nothing.

I hate admitting it, but it's the fucking truth. There are a shit ton of guys out there who would kill, do the unthinkable, cause some serious damage, maybe even sell their mom to the highest bidder to be here right now, in my position. I'm not ungrateful, not by a long shot... I just don't feel anything. Like I said, sometimes this perk, as great as it is, it sure feels like a chore...

Forced.

This is probably going to sound cliché as fuck, but it's not her... it's me. I'm the number one problem in this scenario.

I can put on one hell of a performance.

Putting on a show is one of many things I do best.

My talents are endless, but the truth is, hidden beneath the mask of my ego-tastic bravado, I'm dead on the inside. My dark and corrupted soul is hollow—completely void of any kind of emotion.

Sex...

Sure, it's great and all, but for me it holds zero meaning. It's just another activity I enjoy. It works wonders when I need to de-stress and relax after a grueling training session or a long ass game. If I'm being honest, sex is my go-to. My first choice and favorite kind of coping mechanism. A quick sure way to forget all the hidden demons in my life. A small yet very welcome escape if only for a short while.

A welcome distraction, but that's all it can be.

I'm a guy with needs and I probably sound fucked up, hella crazy but I've never been the deep and meaningful type. I don't believe in love, or sunshine and rainbows for that matter. Happy endings don't exist, and fairy tales are just that... fairy tales. Nothing but a load of bullshit made up in someone's delusional imagination, no doubt to make themselves feel better about their own messed up life.

Life is hard. It's not meant to be easy.

You're brought into this world, and you're forced to play by the cards you've been dealt. You don't make the rules. It's on you to survive. No one else is responsible for whether you win or lose.

I learned from a young age that if you open yourself up, display your heart, exposing it for all to see then you've already set yourself up to fail. I wasn't about to stand back and allow that to happen, so I made a plan. I decided to lock my heart away, completely barricaded, shielded from anything that could potentially make me vulnerable, exposed, potentially hurting me in the process.

Harsh... maybe.

A little drastic, possibly—but it's worked out well so far. Because of my actions and the plan I put in place, I've never experienced any emotional involvement or attachment, and that's cool with me.

Sex is sex... nothing more than a much-needed release.

Growing up, I always thought there was something wrong with me. Some kind of chemical imbalance in my brain, or something deeper like a dodgy genetic defect from birth, but then there lies the start of all my problems.

A story I'll never know.

A story I'll never be told. I'd be lying if I said it didn't bother me from time to time. But as with most things in my life; it is what it is.

I tried to find out where I came from, to learn the story of my roots and my heritage but I was getting nowhere fast. I eventually grew tired and quit searching for something which didn't want to be found. I stopped trying to figure it all out after hitting brick wall after brick wall, and not from lack of trying on my part.

The secrets of my past, whatever they may be, they've been hidden so well it's like they never existed. Like I never existed. I was constantly coming up blank time and time again, so I decided to count my blessings instead. I chose to be thankful for what I did have in my life. It became easy to appreciate the smaller things when I realized I wouldn't find the answers.

The answers I wanted.

The answers I needed.

The answers I deserved.

I shut myself out and silently admitted defeat.

My past is a part of me. A hidden shadow. A part of me I'll never know. Just another thing in a long list of many which I'll be forced to take to the grave with me, buried deep in the earth for all eternity—just the way it was intended.

The curious side of me desperately wanted the answers, but the smarter side of my mind questioned, would it really change or make a difference to the life I'd already worked so hard to create for myself?

Probably not.

I decided it was pointless chasing a non-existent trail, driving myself crazy for no other reason than to stroke my own ego-driven curiosity.

It was high time I stopped dwelling on the past and started to focus on the here and now. On me. I refused to constantly obsess and overthink the endless possibilities. I decided I was broken by default, and there's nothing out there to fix me. There's no magical cure waiting for someone like me.

I'm damaged beyond repair, but these puck bunnies don't seem to mind. They'll take me any way they can get me.

Broken... damaged... whatever. They're still desperate to take a ride on my dick, and who am I to deny them what they want?

CHAPTER TWO
JETT

'Jett...' blondie moans out beneath me, pulling me out of my thoughts, the dark gloomy shadows of my past. I'm really not feeling this tonight. 'Don't stop... oh, God, please don't stop.' She begs as she buckles her small hips, pushing down, desperate to get her fill of me as I continue to take my time, slowly rolling my hips, desperate to feel something... *anything*... but nada. Not so much as a fucking twitch.

I close my eyes and imagine anyone other than the boring blonde on my bed, seemingly having the time of her life as I thrust deeper, selfishly chasing my own release so I can finally draw a line and put an end to tonight's less than victorious conquest.

I shouldn't have picked her up, that much is a given.

I should have finished my drink and walked away, but that's not something I can do easily. I'm the star of this town and I'm surrounded by endless amounts of attention and temptation. Attention validates me and I eat it up like no one else. It fuels my ego, and going home alone would have been totally out of character for me. Something which wouldn't have gone unnoticed either. It's one hell of a catch twenty-two situation.

As usual, I allowed my ego to get the better of me, and to be fair, it sure sounded hella fun at the time, back when I was seven beers deep—but now not so much. Now I can't wait for this shit show to be over.

I'm desperate to claim back my personal space, but I know my role here. I'll persevere and finish the job. After all, I've never been the type of guy who bails. Even when it comes to a boring as fuck pillow princess.

I'll always see things through... Straight to the bitter end. I might be blind when it comes to my origins, but I've always been certain when it comes to one thing. I was born to succeed. I was designed to win at this crazy game we call life and everything in it—no matter what I decide to turn my hand to.

I might be broken, damaged beyond repair, but victory runs freely through my veins. Like a magical elixir.

I also developed one hell of a mean streak over the years too. No doubt a subconscious reaction, making sure I protect myself at all costs against the outside world and anything I can't control. That being said, I'm surprised my dick hasn't deflated and failed me because truth be told, this has to be the worst lay I've had in a while, and believe me, that's saying something.

If there's one thing I hate, one thing which kills the mood real quick, then it's a chick who likes to talk... to have some kind of deep and meaningful during the act. I'm not the type of guy who needs to whisper sweet nothings to get my wicked way.

It's not my style. Never has been, and never will be. I like action and lots of it—on and off the ice.

Sex is a real health boost to add to my already vigorous schedule: never ending training sessions, non-stop workouts and matches, but the second the deed is done, once these easy chicks have served their purpose, I love nothing more than to be left alone with nothing but my own dark and twisted thoughts for company.

Fuck... I need to get blondie out of here and fast. I need to get this cock hungry bitch out of my room before it turns into an epic snore-fest. I force myself to focus on the task at hand, reminding myself that my fuckboy reputation is on the line here. Jett Jameson has never left a girl unsatisfied. But blondie here, she sure feels like an exception to that rule. No doubt the way this is playing out I'll probably end up knocking one out over a porno later to get my fix.

Shit happens but I always try to remain positive.

No matter how bad a situation, there's always a silver lining and porn will forever be my silver lining.

Guess I best hurry up and get this ordeal over with.

Placing both of my hands on her hips, I try to appreciate her naked body; the bounce of her soft creamy breasts one last time as they move freely with each thrust, but her small whimpers of pleasure instantly knock the mojo out of me.

What the fuck is happening to me?

We'll be here all night at this rate. I'll be fucking her until my dick is red raw. A little detail which was never part of the plan. This isn't how my hook-ups usually go. I'm the master of control at all times, and this little blip is knocking me right off balance. I need to get back in the game and fast. I need to snap out of whatever funk I've landed myself in, shift my mindset and get back in the driver's seat.

I pull out, realizing I'm not getting anywhere fast before spinning her small body over in one fluid motion, causing her to scream out, in delight or protest I'm not sure, but I'm way passed the point of caring.

Maybe blondie thinks this is a fun time, but for me it's more like home time. This is one chick who has well and truly outstayed her welcome, for sure. A wicked smirk creeps onto my sadistic lips when I realize this poor deluded little bitch probably thinks I'm switching up positions for her, to maximize her pleasure but that couldn't be any further from the truth.

I already knew this crazy blonde was going to be trouble, and not in the best way. I also knew she wouldn't put up much of a fight. Easy pickings. I mean, where's the challenge? Maybe that's why I'm falling flat—making it real hard to end this disaster. It has to be.

She's been desperate for my dick for months, maybe even longer. Always hanging around training, loitering around my classes. This chick has been following me around, on and off campus, putting herself out there, hoping I'd finally notice her amongst the masses. Desperate for me to take her home. I guess for this lucky blonde her perseverance has paid off— for me, not so much. Now she's currently living her best life and I feel like I've been thrown into a parallel universe.

What should have been a night of fun is slowly turning into the mother of all headaches.

A headache I never fucking wanted or needed.

Personally, if I knew then what I know now, I would have settled for a wank.

This girl, as nice as she might be to the people who know her, she just isn't challenging enough for me. I knew she'd have me any way she could get me—the same as every other chick. Blondie seemed easy enough, yet here we are. I'm about to bust my balls finishing up, and all she can do is lie here like a damp fucking towel.

Chicks man. They're on a whole different level.

Without another beat, blondie throws her hair over her shoulder and as she looks at me I see her wide blue eyes sparkling with excitement before eagerly dipping her back, waiting for me to fill her hungry little pussy again.

This is fucking torture, and not in a good way. I try to focus all my attention on the task at hand, getting this over and done with, focusing solely on my end game.

Keeping one hand steady on her hip, I position my miraculously solid dick at her glistening entrance. When I'm perfectly lined up, I slide my hand up her back, quickly coming to a stop at the nape of her neck, before pushing her unsuspecting head down into my black satin sheets.

Blondie lets out a startled moan of protest and I choose to ignore her. I've listened to her more than enough already and I can't take any more. The sound of her whiny voice is the mother of all cock destroyers. Plus, this is my room and I make the rules.

If she doesn't like it then she can take her wet little pussy out of here. I'm sure as hell not going to put up a fight and stop her. The way I'm feeling right now, I'll probably thank her for leaving me alone.

Eye contact while getting down and dirty is a serious hard no for me.

Eye contact means connection—connection for when two souls become one. When they merge together, and I'm not into that kind of fuckery. I don't do connections, period... and some random puck bunny isn't about to change that.

Hundreds have tried before her and each and every one of them have failed miserably.

This wicked beast... he'll always be untamable.

Another small breathless moan escapes her, muffled by the sheets as I slide back inside her, plunging deeper as I pull her small back into me, completely filling her to the hilt, until I can't get any deeper.

I watch with a notorious smile as her hands grip the sheets, another orgasm imminent, building steady, ready to rush through her exhausted body, and by some miracle my dick pulsates, throbbing violently as her tight walls squeeze around me, almost milking me dry.

This is it...

This is the moment I've been searching high and low for. A moment I was starting to believe would never arrive and I'd be left fucking this boring blonde for the rest of my living days. Not that she'd mind all too much, but personally I couldn't think of anything worse.

Trapped, forced to fuck one and only one pussy for the rest of my days sounds like my own kind of personal hell.

Knowing the end is near, I grip hold of her waist, slowly building the perfect rhythm. My hips move steadily, grinding against her at an even pace, my balls happily slapping her swollen lips, clapping me on, eager for me to reach the finish line.

I don't stop.

I clear my mind and refuse to think of anything else until I've reached my own climax, no longer caring if blondie is joining me for the ride. She's sure had her fair share of fun tonight anyways.

Usually I'd put in more of an effort but I already knew this was a wasted attempt the second she stepped out of her panties. Everything about her was all kinds of wrong, but I didn't have the heart to tell her that she wasn't doing it for me.

Against all odds, I was raised correctly and I was always told if I didn't have anything nice to say then I probably shouldn't say anything at all. But that doesn't matter now. The deed is done. I can put another meaningless notch on my bedpost and be done with it. There's not much point me trying to over-analyze the specifics. One thing I do know is that Blondie needs to go and she needs to go now.

Call me a jerk all you like, but I don't think twice about pushing her sweaty naked body away from me and she collapses face down on the bed, totally spent after receiving too much of the Jett Jameson experience. Not that there was all too much to shout home about for me.

I'm dizzy as a wild rush of relief sweeps through my body. Relief at knowing my night with blondie is finally over—never to be repeated again. It's moments like these where I'm thankful I've always lived by one rule.

Don't fuck the same chick twice.

By all means, have your fun and then forget them... as though they never existed. There's no reason to make these situationships complicated.

I never dip, rinse and repeat.

Some people refuse to wear the same outfit twice. Well, my dick doesn't wear the same pussy twice. Everyone has their own individual standards and that's mine.

Plus, there's no need for me to double dip. Not with the amount of pussy I have on tap. It's a constant flow; an endless stream—one which never runs dry.

Maybe my new roommate will be up to the challenge. I could sure use a new wing man. One who can appreciate the beautiful gift of my cast offs. One who would be more than happy to welcome my damaged goods.

Mason used to be the man; my ride or die, but now the sad-sap has gone and found himself a girlfriend over the summer. He's been pussy whipped and now all the fun has been sucked out of him, no doubt literally through his dick.

'Jett...' blondie murmurs and my blood runs cold. I push myself up off my bed in a heartbeat, quickly putting some much needed space between the two of us before this crazy chick gets way ahead of herself. Before she fools herself into thinking she can change me too.

'Feel free to let yourself out.' I tell her unresponsive body. I'm not all too worried about her comatose state. This is a common occurrence. One which happens more often than not. All they need is a couple of minutes to collect themselves and they'll be fine. I don't have time to stick around and wait for her to come back to the land of the living.

Bad news, sweetheart. I think to myself. *Jett Jameson doesn't do sleepovers,* and even if I did, she sure as hell wouldn't make the cut.

I take one last look at her, splayed out, butt naked on my sheets, clearly in no mad rush to leave. I shake my head and turn towards the bathroom, eager to shower and wash away all traces of her scent and bodily fluids from my skin.

I'm not a gentleman. But then I don't think I've ever claimed to be. I'm Just here for a good time, and I'm quick to remind myself that the new academic year is finally upon us.

A semester with plenty of new conquests, and a wicked grin spreads across my face... blondie instantly forgotten.

CHAPTER THREE
MILA

Once upon a time...

There lived a young girl, hidden away in a small, secluded town. She was trapped, held against her will at the hands of her wicked alcoholic mother. The girl had no viable means of an escape, but that never stopped her from daydreaming, even on her darkest days, and of those there were many. She always somehow found it deep within herself, while surrounded by a blanket of negativity, she somehow found a way to remain positive.

She genuinely believed there had to be something better in this life.

The girl lost herself in her studies and dreamed day and night of nothing but a beautiful escape. With each day that passed she grew tired and more frustrated at the hideous cards she'd been dealt. Growing more desperate to find a miraculous way to break free—free from the painful chains of her mother's prison.

She willed away the days, envisioning her future. One so different from her past and present. A whole new life where she could live freely, and on her own terms. Some place new, anywhere so long as it was far away from this small, miserable town which has done nothing but shelter her.

Never allowing her a single moment to shine or be her true gentle self.

Instead, she was forced to remain hidden, an empty shell of her true potential, like a butterfly trapped in its cocoon, forbidden to change, grow or use its wings. It's the rightful path to a beautiful new life.

The girl wished longingly for wings so she could fly away. She prayed... She wished upon every star... and she prayed some more. The girl prayed so hard to all and any God's in the hope that they would hear her and bestow their mercy.

The girl knew deep down, right in her heart of hearts, that her time would finally come. It might not be today or tomorrow, but fate would eventually intervene and set her free.

Whatever punishment she was carrying from a previous past life would eventually pass. Again, she didn't know when, but she believed with a fierce passion that she needed to remain positive, to keep her vibrations as high as possible and trust in the universe—and herself.

This brave little warrior princess had experienced many battles.

Some she'd won, others she lost with only a bunch of scars to remind her. Yet she still remained determined, and fiercely independent. Traits her mother could only dream of. The girl had plans—big plans and she had every intention of making it out of that small town alive, and she'd make sure she did it alone.

Throughout all the negativity in her life, she was far from naïve. She was headstrong, and she wasn't foolish enough to wait around for Prince Charming to come rushing in on a noble steed to save her.

This fierce warrior princess didn't believe in happy ever after.

She'd witnessed enough destruction and pain over the years to know that true love doesn't exist. It's nothing more than some crazy make-believe fantasy reserved for movies and romance novels.

But if push comes to shove and she has to pick someone, her loyalties will always lie with the Beast every time. A villain with no hidden agenda. The Beast was her guy and she would happily spend the rest of her days with him than any Prince Charming.

The Beast wasn't a superhero, and he never claimed to be. He was a villain and proud. He never pretended to be anything other than his dark true self. You either loved him or hated him—there was no in between, and this brave warrior princess loved him. Oh how she loved him so...

She didn't believe in fairy tales, but out of all the made-up fantasies, he was the only one who would come close to being real. He was more human than people gave him credit for.

He was unapologetic. He wore his punishment with pride. Like a shiny badge of honor... the same way the girl would wear hers with her freedom.

My phone buzzes to life, dragging me out of my usual daydreams and reluctantly smacking me straight back into my hideous reality. A heavy sigh ripples through me when I cast my eyes toward my phone and see the caller I.D.

I haven't been in my car for five whole minutes and she's already on my case. What do I have to do to catch a break around here?

Against my better judgement, I reluctantly picked my phone up and hit the connect button, instantly regretting taking the call. 'Whatever it is, it's gonna have to wait.' I bite out through clenched teeth. A low crackle fills the speakers as it connects to Bluetooth. 'I won't be long. I just need a favor...' the voice demands, instantly getting my back up. A voice which has zero fucks to give. Zero fucks that I'm the one constantly busting my ass off to provide for her and her bad habits.

'I can't talk right now.' I reply, my voice clipped and void of any emotion. I'm not sure why I feel shocked. This is my mom we're talking about, and she's been asking for favors as long as I can remember. Favors which she never returns or appreciates and my patience is growing thin with her never-ending bullshit.

'Mila... are you there?' She calls out into the void and my hands instinctively tighten on the wheel, my knuckles turning white. 'Can you hear me?'

'I hear you.' But I really wish I didn't. 'I'm just busy, mom.' I tell her, trying to keep my voice light and calm, knowing if I show my true feelings and jump on the defensive it will only make her worse. As usual though my mom doesn't care what I have to say, refusing to back down. My mom won't stop until she's got whatever it is she's calling me for.

My mom has serious issues and she refuses to accept that I have a life, no matter how small and inadequate it is outside of her deluded alcoholic bubble which she loves to fester in.

Welcome to my life... the way it's always been. Some fucking fairy tale, right? The truth is, I'm the little girl in my daydreams. I love to imagine I'm a wicked brave warrior princess but here in the real world, I'm nothing more than a defenseless prisoner in her miserable and shallow life.

Is it really wrong for me to want more, to believe I deserve more than this town and what it has to offer?

'I'm not asking for much, Mila...' when I don't respond, a heavy sigh crackles down the line which only angers me some more. I'm already regretting taking the call.

'I'll call you later mom. When I'm finished with work.' I add for additional clarity, not that her selfish brain will register it.

'I can't wait that long.' she hisses as I pull off the highway which connects Coldwater and Ravendale, and the thick downpour grows heavier on my windscreen. The sheets of rain are coming down so fast that my old, battered wipers struggle to keep up. I should probably pull over until it subsides, but then I'd be late for my shift as I'm running on minutes as it is.

If I don't make my shift, I don't get paid, and if I don't get paid then that's a recipe for disaster and then some. Plus, I hate being late for anything. If I'm not where I need to be when I need to be then everything turns to shit and has a knock-on effect on the rest of my day—or night.

To be fair, this is probably only the start of the downpour so I'm best-off driving to work before it gets worse.

'You're gonna have to wait.'

'Seriously?' She pauses a beat. 'Why do you always have to go and make a big deal out of everything? It's always dramatics with you.'

I know what she's doing.

My mom is doing what she does best. She's goading me, desperate for me to give her some kind of reaction, but that isn't going to happen. Instead, I choose to ignore her and her vicious mouth. 'Mom, what are you struggling to understand?' *Life no doubt*, but I keep that thought to myself.

'I'm about to start work.' I pinch the bridge of my nose between my thumb and forefinger and inhale deeply, trying to remain calm and composed when all I want to do is scream. Its proving to be a really grueling task.

My mom is fully aware why I'm not at home right now. She knows all too well that I'm the one who goes out to work. To bust my ass off at our local diner—not her. The supposedly grown ass adult in our fucked-up relationship.

I've been working at Frankie's diner for just over eighteen months and I love it. I love it a whole lot more than I thought I would. Plus, a little independence never hurts anyone. Maybe my mom should try it sometime. Yeah right... there's more chance of her getting sober and staying sober than that ever happening.

The tips sure come in handy too. A little extra I don't need to disclose to my mom. But it's not about the money... not really. I live for the measly few hours I get to myself, the few hours I can finally escape the suffocating confines of our small apartment. Most of the time, my alone time always ends up ruined—ruined by the woman who birthed me into this messed up world.

I'm eighteen, almost nineteen, yet this woman, she manages to keep her poisonous, vicious claws rooted deep into my skin, refusing to let go... *'But not for much longer.'*

'I'll be back in a couple of hours. We can talk then.' I lie effortlessly as I try to pacify her, desperately trying to get this crazy woman off my back for a little while.

'A few hours?' She exclaims, her whiny voice screeching down my speakers. 'A few hours isn't good enough, Mila.' She demands some more, like her tone is about to make me turn around and head straight back home. Not gonna happen.

'No, mom. You don't need me.' I quickly correct her as a wild, uncontrollable rage bubbles deep in my veins. 'You just want something from me.' It's always the same old predictable scenario with her. My mom always wants something from me.

I roll my eyes as the rain continues its unapologetic assault on my truck, pouring down in heavy sheets, showing no mercy. It's pretty ironic how aptly it's reflecting my current situation and mood.

'I don't know where I went wrong with you.' She seethes some more, her true colors finally breaking through her fake ass persona. 'You know, I didn't raise you to be such a self-entitled little bitch.'

Her words sound out around my truck on a heavy slur.

Typical. Fucking typical. It's no secret there's no love lost between me and my mom, but her words still hold the power to break through my protective barriers and slice my unhealed wounds open some more. It stings and burns, each word like a layer of salt thrown onto them, purely to remind me of what she's capable of.

I shouldn't be too surprised. Not really. This happens all the time and I knew it would only be a matter of time before my mom's poisonous tongue came out to play.

If there's one thing about my mom, it's that she's hella predictable and then some. This woman has zero shame. She won't think twice about begging. She'll plead with just about anyone to try to get her next fix. But the moment she realizes she isn't about to get her own way, when things don't go in her favor and that reality slowly filters through her alcohol induced haze, that's when the real Natalie Daniels comes out to play.

My mom, she turns real nasty. I'm more than used to her wicked games and callous antics. I've had years of firsthand experience when it comes to her bullying and vindictive ways. I'm the one who has been forced to live through and endure years of her bullshit... years of her excessively abusing alcohol and whatever else takes her fancy.

I don't know how, but somehow, I've managed to stay strong and pull myself through it. I was the one who held her hair back over the toilet, all through the night, regardless of whether I had school the next day. It was me who had to force my fingers down her throat when she'd had too much, making sure there was nothing left in her stomach so she wouldn't choke an aspirate.

It's fair to say I've grown a thick skin over the years. I've had to grow up before my time, but even now, after all the pain, heartache and sleepless nights she put me through, her vicious attacks, her war of words still hold the power to disarm me.

'Why the hell couldn't I land a decent parent?' Just one. A parent who would naturally nurture and protect me. One who chose to put me first and wanted nothing but the best for me?

Instead, I ended up having a no show for a father and a selfish, heartless monster for a mother. A woman who hasn't raised me. No, I had to do that all by myself, while trying to look after her at the same time. What thanks did I get? Absolutely none. Instead, this woman has treated me with zero respect, dignity, or care.

I am nothing more than a cash cow to her. I always have been, and if I don't get out of Coldwater soon, I always will be.

'I'm not having this conversation when you're being like this, mom.' I begin, trying my hardest to stand my ground, but my mom, as stubborn as she is, decides to cut me off as usual.

'I just need you to come back and give me fifty bucks.' She presses, refusing to back down.

'Fifty bucks?' I exclaim. 'I literally Just paid the electricity bill. What the hell do you need fifty bucks for?'

'All right. Quit with the questions and call it thirty.' Is she being for real? My mom is crazy thinking she can barter with me. I don't care if she goes down to five bucks, she still isn't getting it.

'Not gonna happen.' I bite back, hating with a passion that this woman is still able to get to me. Food... sure, no problem. I'll happily fill up my mom's cupboards all day long, but that's not why she's asking me for money. The cupboards are stocked because I made sure to buy the groceries yesterday. I paid the electric bill today so the supply didn't get cut off. Right now, my mom doesn't need money for anything—except for alcohol.

There's no freaking way I'm about to give her cash, my hard-earned cash just so she can go and waste it all on alcohol. If I do then I'm as good as killing her myself, with my bare hands. It might sound harsh but believe me, that's where she's headed.

My mom is on a drunken downward spiral and she can't even see it.

'Oh, I should have known you'd be too busy to help me out.' She hisses some more. 'You always look out for yourself though, don't you?' Her venomous words roll freely from her tongue on an endless slur. 'All you care about is yourself.'

'Excuse me.' I demand, quickly losing any sense of composure, or the little I have left. 'Are you being for real right now? All I ever do is look out for you and make sure you're good. I wipe your ass daily and this is the thanks I get?'

I feel the heat of my anger rush to the surface, my composure threatening to break completely. Breathing in deep, I decide to be the bigger person and ignore her remarks. I point blank refuse to allow my mom to invade and change my energy—refusing her the chance to get the better of me. I'm so much stronger than this. 'I'm the only person who actually tries to help you and handing you money sure as hell isn't the answer.'

'Yeah, whatever. Sure, you help me out but only when it suits. Only when you've sorted yourself out first. I'm nothing but an afterthought to you.'

Wow... projecting her own insecurities much. I'm not doing this. No way am I going to sit here in the middle of a rainstorm and listen to her drunken word vomit. I am so done with this woman constantly playing the victim. I'm done with her trying to drain my time and energy. She oozes negativity like the plague—drunk or sober.

'I don't have time for this, mom. Unlike you, I don't get to sit on my ass all day. I have a job to get to. I have responsibilities.' Responsibilities which should be hers to deal with, yet here we are. 'So how about you leave me alone for a little while? Better still, why don't you try waking that deadbeat who's no doubt passed out beside you.'

'Mila...' she tries to warn me, but it falls flat. My mom has pushed me way too far this time.

'Mila nothing. Get deadbeat Dan to dig deep in his pockets for a change. Let's see if he's happy to part with fifty bucks.' Dan doesn't have two cents to rub together and my mom sure as hell knows it too, but she's too far gone. Way too deep down the rabbit hole to care. I'll be honest, I'm totally baffled as to why she still keeps him around. I mean, the guy's nothing to look at. He has zero ambition. He brings nothing and I mean nothing to the table. They're both off their heads whenever they're together. It makes zero sense... at least to my mind, anyway.

'Don't you dare talk to me like that, young lady.' I shake my head in disgust and disbelief at her empty words. Her deflated threat. I think it's fair to say that my mom's already consumed her daily dose of alcohol and then some, and it sure sounds like the freeloader is on the beg for some more.

Well, mother dearest can want all she damn well likes, because no matter how loud she kicks off, no matter how loud she screams and shouts, it isn't going to happen, period.

I don't approve of my mom's reckless life choices and nine times out of ten I leave her to her own twisted and delusional devices. Harsh, maybe but she's a grown ass woman—one who actually knows her own god damn mind. If she's hellbent on wasting and ruining the life she's been given then that's on her... and her alone.

I decided long ago that I wasn't playing any part in her downfall. Unlike my mom I have a conscience and there's no way I'm going to willingly aid her untimely demise by ploughing her with alcohol and there's no way I'm giving her money to buy more.

If she's stupid enough to play with fire, then she needs to make sure she's smart enough to douse out the flames. If she's not careful then before she knows it, the fire will eat her up... it's wild and unapologetic frames licking her flesh, burning savagely until she's nothing but ash.

My mom, she's unbelievable at the best of times. She refuses to see or acknowledge that she has a problem. A big fucking problem. Instead, all she sees is people, myself included, thinking we're out to get her. Out to ruin her fun. She's totally intolerable. But when you throw alcohol into the mix, and God knows what else she's taking when Dan is on the scene, she's a recipe for disaster.

She's a woman on self-destruct mode and no one can get to the safety switch to save her. Not even me—her only child. The only piece of family she has left. She's like a petulant child and as harsh as it sounds, her downfall is all her own doing. Personally, I can't wait to see the back of her.

'You want to remember who brought you into this world, Mila... And I'll take you straight back out of it in a heartbeat.' She clicks her fingers together while issuing her usual threats. 'Just like that.'

I've heard enough. I don't think twice about disconnecting the call. I know all too well how this story plays out. I've been here many times before. I know the longer I sit here and listen, the longer I give her the airtime, the worse her insults will become and I'm so not here for her drama.

Not anymore.

She'll keep ringing though. Relentless in her pursuit, hoping if she keeps trying, constantly hounding me then I'll eventually crack under the pressure, eventually giving into her demands and admit defeat.

My mom thinks she'll be able to break me down, make me vulnerable so I'll do anything she wants just to keep her quiet. Like I said, she's predictable and then some.

But that was how things used to be.

I quickly remind myself that I no longer have to answer to her—not anymore, and the feeling is completely foreign to me. Totally new, but I already know it's a feeling I can get used to. One I can quickly adjust to. A beautiful feeling, one which I will cherish for all eternity.

This is my time—my now.

I'm going to take these few hours of freedom I get while working at Frankie's to distract myself. To busy my mind, while effortlessly putting my mom and all her dramas to the back of my head. At least until I'm forced to deal with her bullshit when I get back home.

I seriously deserve some kind of honor or medal for dealing with her for all these years, but I'll happily settle for a guaranteed escape.

Three days.

Three agonizing yet short, glorious days and I won't have to deal with that woman anymore.

I won't have to share a small, confined space with her... at least not on a daily basis anyways and that sounds hella perfect to me.

I am finally walking, albeit baby steps toward my freedom. A wild crazy thought which still manages to send my head into a total spin. I still have to pinch myself at least ten times a day just to make sure it's real; that this is really happening to me and it's not one of my never-ending daydreams.

My mom might have pissed me off, gotten deep under my skin the way only she can but I still can't stop the goofy ass grin as it spreads across my face. I have zero control over it, and I wouldn't want too either.

Last I checked it wasn't a crime to be happy, and I cannot wait to feel the heat of this crazy euphoria all the time. A permanent welcome feature to my day.

No worries...

No stress...

No anxiety...

No alcoholic mother breathing down my neck every five minutes. This is it... it's finally happening. I spent a lifetime thinking I'd be stuck here, trapped in Coldwater forever. A speck of dust in a world full of endless possibilities. Nothing for anyone to remember me by. I spent the majority of my childhood feeling like I'd never be lucky enough to catch a break, and I was never told otherwise.

I was convinced I was the next in line to face the never-ending cycle of generational curses, unable to break the bond—the destiny of my fate.

And why would a little girl think any different when my mom raised me on vicious threats and negative energy? She convinced me I was born to be miserable. Destined to be a failure—just like her.

Never in my wildest dreams did I ever allow myself to think I'd be given the chance... the opportunity to get out of this small, miserable town, but just look at me now.

I swear, I'd give absolutely anything to show my younger self just how far we've come.

It might sound cliché but I don't care. I am living proof if you work hard, if you put in the effort and determination then you really can achieve anything you want to achieve in this life.

My phone buzzes to life again, just like I knew it would, only this time I don't bother checking the caller I.D. I know my mom will be on the other end and I'd rather save myself the headache. I allow it to ring off, knowing all too well that I'll be forced to face her soon enough.

CHAPTER FOUR
MILA

I take a right into Frankie's and kill the engine as a loud clap of thunder rumbles straight above me. I throw my head back against the head rest and close my weary eyes. Taking a much-needed moment to myself.

I listen to the sound of the rain, falling down, splattering against my truck, absorbing the electric energy around me, allowing it to soothe and clear my cluttered mind.

It's always raining in Coldwater. Thats' probably the only thing you can rely on around here—the shocking weather. I hate being out in the rain, the feeling of cold wetness on my skin almost sends me over the edge, but if I'm inside, warm, and dry then I'm more than happy to sit back and listen to mother nature doing her thing. Allowing it to cleanse my soul and wash away all my worries.

I snap my eyes wide open when I feel like all my chakras have been realigned and back at one with the universe and focus on my next move.

Reaching up, I flip down the sun visor and take in my reflection, barely recognizing the girl looking back at me. Dark circles are evident under my big hazel eyes; a sure sign I'm stressed and overtired, but one day soon, I'm hoping that will be a thing of the past.

My long dark lashes are by far my best feature, followed closely by my pink plump lips. My honey blonde hair is effortlessly styled in a long bob of natural waves—effortlessly being the exception here because I don't have enough time on my hands to style it. I just about manage to wash it, allowing it to dry naturally and I'm happy to call that a win. I'm without a doubt the least high-maintenance person anyone will ever meet. And to be honest, I prefer it this way. The last thing I need is an over complicating routine taking up my free time, which up until recently has been extremely limited.

Gliding a small amount of gloss over my lips, I decide I'm about as presentable as I'm going to get. Now, I might not like my mom and her reckless lifestyle choices, but my mom sure blessed me with her good parts. Not that I'd openly ever admit that to her. At least I can be thankful I got her looks and not her reckless personality. There's only enough room in our family for one of us to be so selfish and dependent.

Bracing myself to face the storm, I take in a deep breath and jump out of my truck, straight into the icy sheets of rain. My breath catches from the shock of the sudden assault, and I scream out in protest.

'Fuck...' I cry out as I fall into the mother of all puddles and an instant rush of arctic water crashes up to my calves. My jeans are soaked and I'm almost certain my flats are destroyed—totally saturated. Great... this is just what I needed. Thankfully this is something I'm used to, so I always make sure I keep a spare set of clothes in my lock up at work, but it's still a total ball ache.

What a great way to start my shift.

I don't have much time to dwell on my dose of bad luck as I rush toward the diner door, and I make it over the threshold just in the nick of time.

'One of these days you'll miss cutting it fine.'

'Sorry, Malc.' I offer him a small smile as an icy shudder runs through my body and the cold causes my teeth to chatter. Pulling my jacket tight around my body I move my wet legs across the black and white tiles, eager to get to the bathroom so I can change into warm, clean clothes. 'Mom trouble.' I confess on a small groan, and a look of pity floods his face.

I watch as Malc holds his hands up in surrender as he replies, 'Say no more.'

Everyone in Coldwater and no doubt a few towns over know all about Natalie Daniels and the vicarious life she likes to lead. They know my mom for all the wrong reasons. Just another reason to add to my long list of many to move out of Coldwater.

'I'm sorry.' I apologize again. I know I'm not responsible for my mom or her actions, but I have a conscience and a small part of me still feels responsible for her. Sure, my mom's a grown ass adult, but no matter how hard I try to stay strong, to keep my head held high, my mom will always be a heavy burden I'm forced to carry around with me.

'Seriously, don't sweat it.' His warm brown eyes are curious as they assess me, clearly picking up on my building anxiety. 'It's been pretty quiet anyways. I've been manning the joint just fine.'

'Where's Darla?' I ask, casting my eyes around the diner, noticing the black leather booths are pretty vacant and there's no other staff around.

'She called in sick about an hour ago.'

This surprises me. 'What, on a Friday?' Is Darla crazy? If she is sick then I'll give her my sympathy, but my hidden senses are telling me she's had a better offer and decided to call in a sickie, dropping me in the shit. Right now, it's not too much of a problem. Frankie's is quiet at the moment, but we all know how Friday's play out around here. In the next thirty minutes or so this place will be unrecognizable. The booths will be bursting at the seams and I'm the one who's going to be rushed off my feet, busting my ass as usual.

'I'll go get changed before the masses descend upon us.' I laugh, a ripple of nerves flooding through my body as I look down and take in the sight of my soggy clothes. Friday nights always get busy at Frankie's, and I want to make sure I'm as comfortable as possible before the madness takes over. Before the rush consumes me.

Some people hate it when it's busy. People like Darla who decide to pull a fast one in the hope it goes by unnoticed. Me, I prefer it when it's busy. Time passes evenly, naturally, at a beautiful rate when I don't have a moment to think about anything outside of these red and black walls.

Plus, the tips are always pretty impressive too.

It doesn't take me all too long to slide out of my cold wet clothes and step straight into my warm clean ones, and before I know it, I'm heading straight back out into the diner again, and I breathe out a small sigh of relief when I see the crowd has picked up some.

Reaching out, I grab my trusty pink apron from behind the counter and place it over my head before pulling the strings tight behind my back. I've got this. The moment I slide into my apron, work mode is officially activated. All that's left to do now is paint on my best fake smile and throw all unwelcome thoughts of my mom to the back of my mind, where I will them to stay for as long as possible.

She has no place here.

I come to Frankie's to work and to earn a little extra cash. I come here to clear my mind. Like my own kind of therapy. To enjoy some much needed me time and I'm not about to waste a single second of it. Heated debates with my mom in my head, or in person have no place here. They don't exist in the safe confines of Frankie's.

'What are you doing here?' A small figure approaches my peripheral and when I look up from loading the dishwasher, I see my best friend on the other side of the counter, eye-balling me, suspicion dancing on her heart-shaped face as she pulls her petite body up onto a stool. Her brown eyes are unusually wide, and she's looking at me like I'm about to catch on fire.

'What did I miss?' I question. 'Am I supposed to be somewhere else?'

She taps her manicured nails on the bar impatiently before she bites down on her bottom lip. 'I thought you'd be at home packing up the last of your things.'

Now it's my turn to laugh. I shake my head, unable to stop the carefree grin from spreading across my face, a rush of victorious pride pulsating through my body. 'Come on, Skye. You out of all people should know I've been all packed and good to go for weeks.' She nods her head back at me, like she shouldn't have expected anything else from me. 'Now all that's left for me to do is hit the road.'

'Shit... it all seems to have come around so fast.' She's not wrong, but at the same time D day has also felt like a total drag sometimes too, but that's more of a traumatic response to my own messed up mind.

'You gonna miss me?' I tease, trying to lighten the mood, while also trying so damn hard to keep my shaky voice calm and steady, but on the inside, there's a wild tsunami of emotions crashing through me and I'm really struggling to keep a handle on them.

Her big brown eyes, as familiar as my mind, focus solely on me and her bedazzling smile lights up her whole face; making my best friend look more radiant than usual. I know she's happy for me. I can see nothing but pure pride staring back at me and if the roles were to be reversed, I know I'd be exactly the same.

Me and Skye, were more than best friends.

There's an invisible string holding us together, bonding us, keeping us together through all walks of life. Through thick and thin. We're twin flames, part of the same soul. Soul sisters.

It's no secret that Skye is the one person who has kept me sane over the years, and now suddenly she'll no longer be a stone's throw away. I'd be lying if I said our separation wouldn't be hard, but deep down we both know this is something I need to do.

If Skye was leaving, packing up and escaping the miserable confines of Coldwater, dead set on chasing her dreams, I'd be rooting for her like no one else. Her dreams are my dreams. Her success is my success—that's how we've always worked. But hidden deep beneath the excitement I know she'll be feeling sad too.

We've been inseparable since we were five. I'm not even exaggerating when I say Skye has been the only decent thing to happen in my life, and I'm gutted; totally soul destroyed that I'm going to be leaving her behind.

'Miss you?' She splays a perfectly manicured hand over her chest and her flawless brows pull together. 'Does a bear shit in the woods?'

'Sometimes...'

She rolls her eyes dramatically. 'Of course, I'm going to miss you. I'm going to be lost without you... my mind is still refusing to acknowledge and accept that this is actually happening.' Skye pouts back at me and a small twang of guilt flutters deep within my chest. 'I mean, what am I supposed to do? How am I going to survive without seeing you every day?'

I know exactly how she's feeling. This will be the first time we've spent any time apart in over thirteen years. It's gonna be hella strange, but no matter how hard the transition is going to be, it's a process which needs to happen, and I know we'll both come out the other side a whole lot stronger for it.

I hate seeing Skye getting all upset and down and I try to lighten the mood some more. 'Are you being serious?' A small laugh leaves my lips which helps me sound all calm and collected. Skye's dramatics are something I'm for sure going to miss. 'I'm only a thirty-minute drive away. I'm not up and leaving to travel to the other side of the world, Skye.' Although I have to admit it does kinda feel like that, and not in a bad way.

'You may as well be.' She pouts.

'Whatever.' I bat away her worries and quickly remind her that we're in the twenty-first century now. 'We have technology... Like facetime.' It does absolutely nothing to ease her sour mood and her perfect pout remains on her cherry red lips.

'I know what you're trying to do, and I appreciate it, but facetime isn't the same. Not really. You can try to make this sound all cool, exciting, and technical as you like, but it doesn't change anything.'

'I have a ride, Skye. Just imagine we go to different schools, because when you think about it, that's the only thing that's about to change. Everything else will stay the same —or as good as...

She watches me, a look of defeat swimming in her eyes as she drops her head, her chin falling into her waiting palms, her elbows propped up on the counter. 'I'm just gonna miss having my bestie around, is all.'

A shiver of gratitude ripples down my spine. I've never had reason to be thankful for much in my life, but Skye has always been my one exception. My one exception for everything. Reaching out across the bar, I place my hand on hers and give her a reassuring squeeze—for both Skye and me.

'I'm going to miss you too...'

'Oh yeah... how much?' She questions.

'Too much, but I have it on good authority that you'll still be seeing heaps of me anyway.'

'Are you trying to be funny?' She demands, her voice clipped. 'You know I don't bode well with games, Mila... Don't fuck with my fragile heart because I won't be able to take it.'

Her voice is pleading and a small smile creeps onto my face. 'I'm not playing games. I promise.' I tell her, hoping my news will ease her overactive and oversensitive mind, giving it a much-needed rest. 'I'll still be coming back to Coldwater.'

'What? The whole point of you leaving was to get away from that witch of a mother of yours.'

'I'm not coming back for her...' I allow the words to fall flat around us.

'Then why...' her brows furrow in confusion. 'I don't understand...' she looks cute as hell. I could leave her hanging on the edge of her seat, the suspicion slowly torturing her, but she's been through enough emotional damage at my hands already.

'I'm not leaving Frankie's. I spoke to Malc about the idea a few weeks back, and he's happy to keep me on the books, so long as I don't burn myself out along the way.'

'Wait...' She gasps, her mouth almost falling to the floor. 'You're not leaving Frankie's?' Skye couldn't hide her relief and excitement even if she tried.

'Nope.' I reply without missing a beat. 'I'm afraid you can't get rid of me that easily. You're still stuck with me... well at least most evenings anyway.'

'Oh my God. I can't tell you how happy I am to hear you say that. I'm relieved, for sure...' her brilliant smile falters a little before a flush of confusion scatters across her face.

'But...' I press, sensing that there's a massive hitch to my plans.

'But... I don't know.' She waves her hand, quickly playing down her concerns. 'I guess I thought you wanted to be out of Coldwater for good. And what about your studies?'

I think on her words for a moment, and I totally get why her mind wandered in that direction and came to that conclusion. I guess to a normal person it would make sense, but I established long ago that I'm far from normal. But the truth is, I need this job. I need the money and above all else, I need the mental stability.

'I've thought about it. Believe me, I have pictured all the different scenario's and I've thought about them long and hard over the past couple of months...' I've never held anything back from Skye and I don't plan to start now. We've always been up front with each other—the way best friends should be. 'I'm desperate to get away from my mom, but not everyone else. 'Plus, you know better than anyone that I'm no good when it comes to change...'

'Say's the one who's actually leaving town in a couple of days. The sarcasm rolls freely from her tongue, but I don't take her bait. Instead, I scowl at my best friend, offended that she's exposing me so freely.

'That's different, and you know it.' I narrow my eyes, warning her to keep her opinions to herself. 'I need to leave so I can give myself a better chance of escaping this hell hole for good. Frankie's... this place has been good for me, you know. This joint was the first place I got a real taste for independence, and even though this town depresses the crap out of me, Frankie's is where I belong.' My chest tightens involuntarily as I say the words out loud, and I mean every single one of them.

'I get that, but what about your studies?' Skye presses. 'Won't it be easier and less time consuming for you if you found a job in Greenmount, or on campus?'

'Sure it would, but when have I ever decided to take the easy route?'

Skye leans back, letting out a dramatic sigh. 'True. I guess I can't argue when you put it like that. Just promise me one thing...'

'Shoot.' I say before I have a chance to regret promising anything.

'Promise me you'll listen to your body. Promise me you won't take on too much.'

'Okay, I promise. But who are you and what have you done with my best friend?'

'I'm being serious here. You're going to be away from home, surrounded by total strangers and the last thing you need is to burn yourself out in the process.'

Seriously. Thats' all she's worried about? I've been burnt out and then some throughout all the years I've had to deal with my mom and her endless bullshit. My studies and a few shifts at Frankie's will feel like a walk in the park. Nothing that's going to break my back.

'Enough about me...' I quickly change the subject. 'What are you doing here, anyways?' If my memory serves me correctly, I'm pretty sure Skye should have been going on a sexy hot date with Ravendale's' very own fuckboy—Shawn Croft. 'I thought you had a hot date.'

'Don't.' She shakes her head. 'You wouldn't believe me even if I told you.'

'Why don't you try me.' I deadpan, refusing Skye a way of wriggling out of an explanation. Initially I was concerned—led to believe Skye and Shawn were the real deal, but I've always been firmly on the fence. I've never been Shawn's biggest fan, but Skye's happiness has always been more important to me. Skye is where my Loyalties lie, and nothing will ever change that.

'I'd rather not talk about it,' her voice is barely a whisper, but I hear her loud and clear.

'Maybe it's for the best.' I offer in my most sympathetic voice. I want my best friend to be happy, but

Shawn seriously isn't it. He gives me the creeps. He's sleazy as fuck, and everyone and their mom knows he's the biggest fuck boy in Coldwater.

Skye bites down on her bottom lip before worrying it between her teeth. 'He cancelled. Apparently, he had some family event he couldn't get out of...'

'Really? Is he expecting us to sit back and buy that bullshit excuse?' Shawn and family aren't a compatible combination. Shawn and family values don't even belong together in the same sentence. I'm surprised he didn't choke on his bullshit excuse. Shawn Croft wouldn't know what family values were if they rocked up, said *'hey,'* and slapped the jerk in the face, but then what do I know? 'Do you believe him?' I ask before I can stop my unsensitive mouth from running away with itself.

'I want to. Really, I do, but I'm starting to think everything you said about him was right.'

'You bet it was. Don't sweat it, because fortunately for a beauty like you, there's heaps more fish in the sea.'

'I don't like fish.' She wrinkles her nose in disgust, and I automatically shake my head at her.

'No, but you like guys, right?'

'Damn straight.' She plasters on her best award-winning smile, all thoughts of Shawn Croft and his dickish antics temporally forgotten. 'Any way, enough about me. How are you holding up, and I mean on a serious level.' Her voice is soft, laced with concern. Skye's spidey senses automatically picking up on my low mood, even though I've been trying my hardest to hide it. Who am I kidding? I've never been able to hide anything from Skye, period, so what's the point in trying now? She's like some kind of superspy, always on the lookout; always knowing. Skye always knows when something isn't sitting right with me.

'I'm good.' I say with zero conviction in my voice, and I already know she doesn't buy it.

'You sure?' Skye is quick to raise a quizzical brow at me. 'Because if it was me packing up and leaving town, destination Greenmount, then girl, you best believe I'd be shouting it from the rooftops.'

Personally, Sunday can't come quick enough. I'm excited for sure, but I'm also hella anxious too.

Sunday is the start of a brand-new chapter for me. A chapter I can't wait to explore. I mean, this is the moment I've been waiting for—the moment, I've worked so hard for, but even now, even after I've seen all the evidence in black and white, it still doesn't feel real.

Pressing my dry lips together I watch Skye closely, quietly confessing. 'I'll be happy when it's actually happening.' I've spent months, refusing myself the feeling of getting too excited. Too caught up in case Greenmount suddenly realizes they messed up. A massive clerical error where my papers have been mixed up with someone else's. I panic every time my phone rings and I don't recognize the number, convinced it will be someone at Greenmount calling to revoke my offer. My whole mind and body have been on pins.

'Oh, it's happening.' Skye reminds me, proving that my doubt is all deep in my mind, yet it does absolutely nothing to ease the wild flutters buried deep inside my chest.

'I know. But until I slam the door shut on my truck and hit the gas, that's when I'll finally let my guard down and exhale a massive sigh of relief. I think that's when it will all hit home for me.' My mind instantly wanders, imagining for the millionth time what my new life will actually look like. And I'd be lying if I said I hadn't had a few nightmares too, convincing myself that there had indeed been some kind of clerical error with my grades, meaning my offer of a place at the prestigious

Greenmount U no longer applied. It will be withdrawn, no doubt, quickly passed onto someone more deserving of a place.

My mind is overactive at the best of times, but knowing my luck, this situation is something that would totally happen to me. I need to switch up my mind set before I unwillingly manifest it into my reality.

'Mila... quit stressing. This is happening and nothing is going to ruin or jeopardize your new adventure.' A knowing smile plays on her lips, and I know she's right. The sooner you accept that you've worked your butt off and made it, and you're getting out of here, the sooner you'll be able to relax and enjoy what's happening.' She beams back at me, shaking her blonde head in disbelief. Under the pressure of her heated glare, I finally crack and allow myself to feel a sense of what I've achieved—achieved all by my little old self. I pause a moment, allowing the rare but delightful feeling of victory and empowerment to sink in and swim freely through my veins.

Skye is right. I have worked so God damn hard to get to where I am, and I should be shouting it from the rooftops. I should be so proud of myself, instead I'm wasting all my energy worrying about people who don't even give a damn about me. Once again, my mom trickles to the forefront of my mind and I use everything I have to put her straight to the back of it again. I'll keep her locked away for as long as physically possible but I know she'll soon rear her ugly head again.

'I'm trying not to think about it too much. Because if I do then everything will happen in slow motion, and I've been waiting for this for an age. Damn, I want Sunday to be here already.'

'And...' She waggles her flawless eyebrows at me.

'And what...' I feel my own brows furrow in confusion.

'Are we going to discuss the elephant in the room? What about Cole?'

The sound of Cole's name falling from Skye's mouth instantly gets my back up and all previous elation which coursed through my body vanishes in a heartbeat. My happy mood is no more. Instead, the dark cloud of doom creeps back in, any hope of my happiness vanishes just as fast as a pair of hooker's panties.

'What about him?' I bite out and I can taste the bitter venom on my tongue. I also don't miss that my voice switches to instant defensive and I know Skye doesn't miss it either. I avoid making eye contact with her and for good reason. Skye has always been able to read me like an open book. She holds the power to see straight through me, so I quickly busy my hands and wipe down the already gleaming countertop. I think this has to be the cleanest it's ever been. So shiny that I can see my complete reflection in it.

'Have you spoken to him?' Skye quizzes.

'Nope.' I emphasize the P so she understands the subject of Cole should be off limits at the moment. But on the other hand, I know it's a pointless feat trying to lie to my best friend. She'll find out soon enough anyway. Cole: Royal Raven's Hockey Captain—my so-called boyfriend has ghosted me for the best part of two weeks. It's almost like he's turned into a different person ever since I told him I made the grades and received my acceptance letter offering me a place at the prestigious Greenmount U. To say he was less than impressed would be the understatement of the year.

I guess I was the one who was foolish enough to think he would have been happy for me. That he would have been proud. Proud of my hard work, my determination, my achievements... especially after everything I've been through over the years. Against all odds, I'd somehow managed to nail all of my exams.

I really thought he would have been happy that I'm finally one step closer to my dream. Although it stings a little... actually it stings a lot. I have to face up to the fact that he's the one who's being unreasonable here. He's the one who can't take a step back out of his glory and find it within himself to be happy for me. But then maybe Cole has always expected me to remain hidden in his shadow... to be unheard and rarely seen.

It makes sense now as to why he started the mother of all arguments. Life was no longer about him and his greatness, and I went from hero to zero in a nano-second.

All forms of his previous support were removed in that moment and his attitude toward me changed. Apparently, even though I always do everything for everyone else, the tables had unknowingly turned. Cole told me that all I ever think about is myself, and the second he'd finished with his word vomit, he didn't stick around to hear what I had to say in response. Instead, he turned around and walked away from me. He didn't even look back as the silent tears fell down my face, leaving a hot salty trail in their wake. And it's been crickets ever since.

'Seriously?' Skye exclaims, dragging me out of my thoughts. 'Not even a phone call. A text?'

'Seriously... none of the above.' I raise my eyes and take in the look of pity reflecting back at me. 'But if he thinks I'm going to stand around waiting for him to come back, then he's in for a shock. I'm not wasting my time on someone who doesn't deserve it.'

'That's my girl.' Skye is ecstatic at the news. 'I always said you were too good for him. He's never deserved you.' She reaches across the bar and jabs my arm, her one and only way of showing me any form of affection, but it's there all the same, and it isn't lost on me.

'Enough of the *'I told you so's.'* I warn her playfully, but on the inside, I'm being deadly serious. Cole's a dick, that much is a given. I don't need Skye to remind me how foolish I've been over the years.

Skye pauses for a moment, silently contemplating what she wants to say to me... weighing up if the good will outweigh the bad. I know this look. It's a look which usually almost always ends in disaster. 'Are you free tomorrow night?'

'I should be why.' I struggle to hide the suspicion in my voice, and I know she doesn't miss it either.

'Hey... don't look at me like that.' She warns, her small brown eyes glistening with danger.

'I'm not looking at you like anything. So, tell me, what's happening tomorrow.'

'I thought you of all people would know, seeing how you're now part of the elusive elite.' She turns her nose up at me in fake disgust.

'You've lost me.' I confess. I have no idea what the hell she's talking about. I shake my head at her, still none the wiser. Whatever she's trying to tell me with her wide eyes, it's sure falling flat.

'How the hell are you going to survive when you actually leave and go to Greenmount?'

'Come on... just spit it out.' I plead, realizing the two of us will be here all night going back and forth, while getting no closer to what's actually going on. 'In case you didn't notice, I'm supposed to be working here...'

'The start of semester Lake party.'

I narrow my eyes at her. 'We've never had a start of semester Lake party.'

'No, we haven't. But now you have.' She sighs dramatically. 'Don't you bother to read anything that Greenmount sends you?'

I think back on all the paraphernalia and information packs I've been sent over the last two months. Yes, I've glanced here and there but to be fair I've had to hide them, so my mom doesn't see them. Anything relating to Greenmount causes her to kick off and I've been trying to avoid her like the goddamn plague. 'Why, when you seem to be doing such an epic job of going through it for me.'

'Well, just be thankful you have a bestie who pays attention to the small things happening in your life. Thanks to me, there's a party with your name on it, and it's happening tomorrow night... and because I'm awesome, it makes sense for me to offer up my services and come along as your plus one.'

'Oh, you did, huh?'

'Of course. Cole isn't on the scene so that's one less piece of baggage to weigh you down, and I know you wouldn't want to miss out on this kind of experience...' She smiles sweetly at me, all angelic like she can do no wrong. Only I know better. she's the devil in disguise. 'It could be like your final send off before you're set free into the big wide world.'

I have to give it to her. God sure loves a trier.

'Do I even get a say?' I laugh, already knowing what her answer will be. Surprisingly, Skye doesn't say anything, only broadens her smile some more. 'Okay, how about I do you a deal.'

'I'm listening.'

'If I say yes, can you please order something before Malc goes bat shit crazy? The last thing I need is him thinking I'm standing her slacking.'

'Damn straight, I'll order whatever you want me to, so long as it grants me VIP status tomorrow.' Now she's pushing it, but I'm not about to say it out loud to her. I need her on side so I'm going to have to play nice—at least for a little while.

'Fine, we'll go to the party.' I'm sure, I'll survive a few hours at the lake. I guess it's a small price to pay to keep Malc off my back. 'Now what are you ordering?' I throw my towel over my shoulder, letting her know I mean business.

'Erm...'

'Whoa... don't mess with me Skye. I need your order, so hurry up and order something fast before I get shown the door.' If Malc decides to wander out of the office and sees me behind the counter, he'll think I'm over here having a whale of a time with my bestie instead of actually working. After all, its' what he pays me to do.

'Have you eaten?'

Not since lunch, and my stomach growls out in protest, but I'm quick to shut it down. 'What do you think? But that doesn't matter. You're the customer here, not me. Or at least you're supposed to be. I'm just a slave, here for your service.'

'Dramatic, much?' She scowls back at me, hating being called out.

'Yeah, sure, I'm the dramatic one. You know I'm always rushed off my feet when I'm working.'

'So, tell the obnoxious prick to stick it.'

'Skye, its fine.' I try my best to calm her before she stands up and makes a scene. 'This is what happens when you work. The answer is in the description. ' I sigh.

'What about that other girl... what's her face? I haven't seen her around for a while. Shouldn't she be in with you tonight?'

'Yeah, Darla. She should be but she decided to pull a sickie at the last minute, so it all falls onto my shoulders, but I can handle it. There's only me here to pick up the slack... unless...' I narrow my eyes before an ear-splitting grin takes over my face. I don't say this often but I'm a fucking genius.

'Wait... what is that?' Skye stammers while pointing a finger at my face. 'Why are you smiling?'

'What if you get a job here too.'

'Are you insane?'

'For once, I don't think I am. Look, it makes total sense. We see each other all the time and you'll get to make a little extra cash on the side...' I watch in silence as she muses over the idea in her mind.

'Mila... I've never worked before.'

'So, everyone has to start somewhere, right? Want me to put in a word for you with Malc at the end of my shift?'

'Are the tips good?' I can't help but laugh. Skye has always been materialistic.

'Sure, if you do a good enough job, they can be decent, but you can't allow that to determine your pay check. I always have my standard amount in my mind and any tips are a bonus.'

'You sure you want to stay working here? I don't want to commit myself to a job if you're not going to be here.'

'I told you already, I'm happy to stay put.'

'But there will be heaps of bars near campus.'

'Are you trying to get rid of me?' My voice is teasing but a flicker of paranoia sparks on the inside.

'Don't be silly. I just thought it would have been more convenient for you, is all.'

'On paper, maybe, but I think I'm best sticking with Frankie's. I'll stick with what I know.' I tell her. 'There's no reason to up and leave here too. I like it here, plus I have a ride and it's only a twenty-minute commute. It makes sense to stay here, plus I'll need all the extra money I can get.' Another reason is I still get to keep a close and watchful eye on my mom and her reckless ways, but from a safe distance.

Theres no way my mom is going to help me out, and my dad... well, he hasn't dipped his hands into his pockets since I was about five, so I won't even bother holding my breath where he's concerned.

Surprisingly, Skye doesn't say anything. All she does is nod back in agreement. She knows better than anyone that I sure as hell didn't hit the jackpot when I was given my parentals.

I look around the darkened diner and see its' busy-ish... still quieter than usual for a typical Friday night, but I don't allow the empty seats to throw me into a false sense of security because I know any second now the masses will descend and I won't get a moment to think again until it's time for me to close up for the night.

'So, are you ordering something or what?' I hastily remind Skye. 'Food, maybe a drink?' I press, eager to get her seated and away from the counter. Malc, my boss... he's more than happy for the kids to come here and hangout, but he gets a little pissed if his girls are seen to be hanging around or gossiping with their friends. Especially if said friends aren't digging deep into their pockets, the money going straight into his cash register.

Malc is a good guy. He's also been known to be kinda cool on occasion too, but he loves nothing more than to keep his diner busy. Busy means money and money makes him a happy guy. Like I said, Malc has no issues with the kids hanging out here so long as they know they have to pay for the privilege. Making sure they pay their keep and all that. So long as they purchase his food and drink, he's as happy as a pig in shit.

Little old me... I'm hired to make sure all of the above happens while he spends his time hidden away in his little office. It's rare for him to be seen out front, unless we're short staffed, like we are tonight. Usually, Skye can hang out for a while before he strolls out of his office, but not tonight. Not when his beady eyes can see everything. And the last thing I need is to lose my job right before I head off into the sunset—destination Greenmount.

'That all depends...'

'On?'

Skye smiles her usual breathtaking smile and I know she's loving every single second of my current discomfort. 'It all depends on whether you're going to take a break and have something to eat with me.'

'Er hello...' I run a hand down my body, 'can't you see I'm working?'

'Obviously I can see that. But there's a legal requirement fitted into every worker's contract and newsflash... you're entitled to a break, Mila.' She pouts, forcing me to back down. I suppose it would be one way to get her off my case for a while, so I decide to meet her halfway.

'I literally just started my shift so I'm not due a break yet but seeing how it's you I'll meet you in the middle. Order a drink for now, and when I'm due for a break we can eat together. How does that sound?'

'Like a dream... and then we can make plans for the Lake party tomorrow night.' She flashes me a victorious grin, knowing she's got me right where she wants me. 'Grab me a coke and I'll go sit by the window.'

I make her a coke and take it over, eager to get to work before Malc has me out of here faster than I'd be able to say sorry.

CHAPTER FIVE
JETT

I kill the engine and climb out of my car, my mind on overdrive as I allow the cool winter breeze to whip around my face and I welcome it, the ice slowly soothing my fiery soul... as I inhale a deep lungful of air, causing my chest to swell as an unusual sense of calm washes over my body.

This is home.

This place right here is where I belong.

Nothing and no one will ever come close to replacing this feeling. Many have tried and each and every one of them have always failed at the first hurdle. It's kinda comical how it never ends. They just keep coming and they keep on trying, relentless in their pursuit.

I look up toward the overcast sky, watching in silence as the storm clouds roll in, while taking a rare moment of reflection as the rain drops start to fall.

Small pitter patters fall down on me as mother nature tries to do the unthinkable; the unimaginable and wash away my sins. A small laugh escapes my lips at the irony. All the water on this earth wouldn't be enough... wouldn't hold the power to wash away my sins.

Nothing can redeem me. Not even God himself. My soul is long gone... way past saving.

I'll be the first to admit I've made my fair share of mistakes in this lifetime, the main one being I don't come home as much as I should do. As much as I used to. But I'm here, trying my hardest to put that right. I'm trying to make more of a conscious effort to be thankful for the ones who have my back. The select few who know the real Jett Jameson. The select few who don't judge me for my faults. Who I can be my true self with... no mask or bravado needed.

To them I'm still the little Kid, curious and wild with the big green eyes. They don't see the hockey god, Greenmount's very own golden boy. They just see me, and it's strange, but a welcome change.

'Baby steps.' I remind myself. Piece by piece, one torturous step at a time. I'm here now and that's what really matters, right?

Slamming the car door behind me, I take one last pull on my smoke before flicking the butt to the ground. It's a nasty habit, one which I can't seem to kick, but what's one more against my long list of many? Surely one more isn't going to hurt. I'm heading straight to hell anyway, so I may as well enjoy the ride.

A wicked smirk creeps onto my lips at the thought before I finally take a step forward and make my way across the gravely driveway, welcoming the crunch under my boots as my childhood home graces my vision. I pause, taking in a deep calming breath and think back to when life was easier. Back when it was so much simpler. Back when I didn't know what kind of deadly demons were hiding deep inside my closet. Way back when my mind was completely oblivious and I didn't even realize I had a fucking closet.

'Jett...' the sound of my mom's voice flows out from behind the red wooden door as I approach and a sudden rush of intense heat radiates from deep within my chest. I can act the big man, for sure... all day fucking long. I can play the ultimate tough guy, but my mom, she holds the power to revert me straight back to being a little boy in a heartbeat.

A moment later the door swings open and she greets me, her warm brown eyes wide with wonder. 'Jett, honey... is it really you?' Her voice oozes disbelief and my guilt intensifies.

'It's me, mom. The one and only...' I laugh, and an instant boost of serotonin blazes through my veins. Her radiant smile lights up her whole face. She looks so happy and carefree, reminding me that for all my many faults, being a selfish self-centered jerk tops that list.

Shit... how did I allow it to come to this?

I didn't realize just how much I'd missed this woman until now and my chest tightens some more, the heavy weight of my guilt slowly rippling through my body, catching me off guard and disabling me, almost crippling my six-foot five frame.

Not an easy feat, for sure.

'Well, don't just stand there, boy.' She beams back at me, not a single trace of anger or resentment, nothing but unconditional love oozing out of her every pore. 'Come here and bring it in.' The small plump woman standing before me, my safe space from a young age throws her arms wide and welcomes me straight back into her warm embrace—like I've never been away.

'When did you get so big?' She demands, squeezing me tighter, just to make sure I'm real and not a figment of her imagination, and I surprise us both when I don't pull away. 'And just like that, in the blink of an eye my baby boy is all grown.' She mutters into my chest, her voice faltering, riddled with emotion.

I continue to stand here, outside my childhood home as my mom keeps a firm, protective hold on me and I decide to use this opportunity to take a moment—a much-needed moment to collect my erratic thoughts and lose myself in this super rare, carefree moment.

I feel my shoulders loosen as all my pent-up anger and frustration slowly begins to ebb away and leaves my body. For a split second all my worries instantly disappear. They vanish into thin air like they never fucking existed.

I'll be honest, I don't know how she does it, but my mom has always been able to soothe any issues, no matter how big or small. This woman; she's the mother of all band aids. She's magical for sure.

I wait patiently, silent until my mom has finally had her fill of me and I allow her to pull back first. When she does, her eyes are still wide, totally amazed that I'm still here and she isn't imagining it. She just juts her small chin, raising her head so she can take a better look at me before placing her hand delicately on my chest, perfectly positioned over my heart. The glisten in her eyes renders me speechless and I force myself to swallow down on the hard lump of raw emotion which forms at the back of my throat.

There's no denying this woman was sent from God. An angel placed here to do good on this horrific place we call earth. One of a kind. A rare fucking treasure and I'll never hear anyone say anything different, period.

I follow her up the stony path, feeling a deep sense of ease. A knowing that no matter what, everything will be alright. Somehow, against all odds, the universe will shift ever so slightly and put some much-needed normality back into my life.

As I step over the threshold, the smell of my mom's homemade cooking and sweet pastries fill the air around us, instantly invading my senses and catapulting me straight back to my childhood, a bunch of hidden memories rushing to the surface.

Some good... some not so good.

I'm not all too surprised to see the floral decor hasn't changed over the past couple of years and as I continue my way down the small hallway, I see the walls are still lined with family photographs.

Another flash back to my past that I wasn't expecting.

Breathing in deep, my chest tightens, crushing in on itself as the nostalgia hits hard, quickly depleting my limited oxygen supply.

What the fuck is happening to me? I'm Jett fucking Jameson. I don't get emotional. I don't have a soul, and I sure as hell don't have feelings, period. I've been back home all of two fucking minutes and I'm acting like a grade A pussy. A pussy who can't keep his shit together.

My stomach growls out in protest and a small chuckle flits in the air between us. 'Don't tell me they haven't-been feeding my boy properly at that place?'

'Sure, they have, mom.' I smile automatically, 'but no one's food can ever compare to yours.' We both know I'm speaking nothing but the truth when I say this.

All traces of a happy reunion instantly vanish as soon as I approach the small kitchen and take in my surroundings.

'Would you look what the cat has dragged in.' A cold malicious voice hisses from the wooden table by the window, instantly getting my back up. I should have prepared myself for this little hitch.

'Sienna... that's no way to greet your brother.' Mom quickly scolds, always taking my side over hers, and she scrunches her heart-shaped face up in annoyance. 'He's just arrived home, so I'm sure you can find it deep within you to play nice for five minutes.'

'Wait,' She wails. 'Why am I suddenly the problem?' Sienna shakes her head in disbelief, her long black hair falling down over her shoulders. 'All I'm doing is voicing my opinion. Pure facts, mom.' She snaps her eyes toward me before narrowing them. 'I'm pretty sure if I disappeared for months at a time without checking in, we'd be having a completely different conversation right now.'

'Sienna...' mom warns again, while somehow managing to keep her voice calm and light. 'Enough.'

Sienna holds her hands up, playing the innocent victim as usual. 'I'm just surprised he remembers he has somewhere to call home instead of fueling his ego on people's pity by making out he's some long-lost forgotten orphan.' She bites out each word and the venom on her tongue is potent—always a lethal dose.

As much as I hate to admit it, her words pierce my armor and sting a little. I'm not stupid. I've never hidden who I am, and I know what she's saying is true. In all fairness, I should have been here, but no one can change the past. Not even a hockey God like me. What's done is done.

I knew Sienna would be pissed. In fairness she's the biggest bitch I know and she's pissed the majority of the time, but I haven't been home for months, maybe even over a year. I've barely called, or checked in to see how they are. Sienna is a sensitive soul underneath the hardened exterior she's forced herself to wear over the years. Me and her; we're more alike than either of us would ever be willing to admit. Knowing Sienna as well as I do, she would have taken my absence to heart. She would have made it personal. An insult, convincing her deluded little mind that I'd decided to sell her out for my newfound family at college. My boys. My teammates. My ride or fucking dies.

I'll be honest though. Sienna is one of the reasons I kept my distance, and she knows it too. Not that I'd ever dream of confessing that little detail to her any time soon, if ever. I'm a guy who values my balls and I'll do what's needed to keep them firmly attached to my body—where they belong.

I should have been ready for her attack. It was stupid of me to come here, totally unprepared, knowing all too well I'd be forced to face the heat of Sienna's wrath. Knowing with time it doesn't ebb and fade. No, with Sienna, her rage intensifies, growing hotter with each day that passes by. She's like a ticking time bomb, and I'm the fool who's just pulled the detonator.

Time has just ran out—on my fucking watch.

Sienna is my sister, but not by blood. She's my mom's daughter through and through, but blood isn't always thicker than water.

Norma, or mom as I prefer to call her, she adopted me when I was around eighteen months old or something. She doesn't like to discuss all the nitty details and I respect her enough not to push the issue. All I know is she dragged me out of a bad situation. This woman saved me, and she's treated me as her own ever since. As far as my mom is concerned, even though she might not have given birth to me, or brought me into this world... she's still my mom no matter what, and words will never be able to fully describe how thankful I am that she chose me.

I cast my eyes toward my little sister and a small smirk pulls at the corner of my mouth. 'It's really good to see you too, Cee.' My voice is like ice, but I try to keep this situation amicable for my mom's sake. I can try to save face for both of us but it's my lack of fucks to give which is going to annoy Sienna the most. 'Did you miss me?'

'Fuck you, dickweed.' She growls back on a hushed whisper so only I can hear her. I smile and her eyes grow wide with fury, but I don't miss the rush of heat flushing her cheeks, displaying her obvious embarrassment.

The last time I made a trip back home I did the big-brotherly thing and told Sienna she could hang out with me, so long as she didn't fuck around.

I thought she'd enjoy getting out of the house. There was a get together happening down at the Lake and what better way to unwind than by kicking back and having a few beers between friends. Nothing out of the ordinary... until Sienna thought it would be a good idea to make a totally unexpected and unwelcome drunken pass at me.

Admittedly it's a well-known fact that I'll fuck anything with a warm and welcoming pussy, but there's times where I'm quick to draw the line... and that line starts and ends with Sienna.

She might not be blood but she's still family, and family is a step too fucking far—even for me.

'Aww, don't be like that, Cee... '

Her blue eyes narrow, filled with a deep hatred as she shoots daggers my way, and I struggle to barrel my large frame through the small kitchen... a kitchen which seemed so much bigger the last time I was here. Pulling out one of the wooden chairs, the closest one to me, one which has seen better days, I lower myself down and try to make myself comfortable. The wood creaks and groans out in protest under the added pressure of my weight.

Sienna doesn't answer me, clearly dead set on being the stubborn bitch we've grown to love and hate over the years, so I flash her my killer smile, knowing my arrogant ego-tastic persona will piss her off some more.

As much as I'd love to retaliate and stoop right down to her childish level, I'm quick to remind myself that I didn't come here to see Sienna. I came home to see my mom, like I should have done months ago. But as usual I haven't been here for all of five minutes and already the diva inside her is causing a scene. The last thing I want or need right now is to get caught up in a fight, or more importantly spending my limited and precious time here finishing one.

I know my mom wouldn't thank me for it.

'Like what?' She snarls, leaning her body over the table so she doesn't have to shout and draw any unnecessary attention to us. 'Am I supposed to be happy to see you? Am I supposed to be okay with you heading out and forgetting about us? Am I expected to accept that you don't want to bother with us anymore?'

'Hey...' I hold my hands up in surrender, trying to calm her down and lighten the mood. 'That was never my intention,' I confess, telling her nothing but the truth. 'I'm a busy guy, Cee. You know how it is.'

'Oh, yeah... being Greenmount's' favorite fuck boy must be really challenging.' The sarcasm rolls freely from her tongue, but I don't mistake the trace of jealousy swimming in her voice, swirling the arctic air around us, but as usual I decide to be the bigger person and ignore her smart-ass mouth.

It doesn't matter what she says or does. It doesn't matter how badly she acts; it won't change anything. No matter how worked up she gets, how pissed she gets, I'm still not going to fuck her. Not even to shut her up. Not now... not ever.

Sienna's just gonna have to find a way to suck it up. The sooner she realizes nothing will ever happen between us, the better it will be for the both of us.

'Like I said, I'm a busy guy.'

'Too busy for family time?' She hurls back with zero hesitation and I don't miss the innuendo heavily laced in her comment. See, the difference is, I know what kind of family time Sienna is thinking about and if mom ever found out the depth of Sienna's intentions, it would kill her. Something that messed up would send mom straight to the grave, for sure, and that's not the kind of blood I'll ever have on my hands. Anyone else, no fucking problem, but not my mom. Never my mom.

'Now, now, you two...' Mom calls over to us, obviously picking up on the heavy atmosphere. She comes to a stop at the table before rewarding us both with her disarming smile.

'Would you just look at my babies, sitting down together at the table. A beautiful sight I haven't seen in way too long.' Her voice catches, riddled with a mixture of pride and emotion. 'Please allow your old mom to enjoy this moment. The last thing I want is for you two to start arguing about this and that, and start tearing my kitchen apart.'

As soon as mom has said her piece, she walks back over to the stove—the one place she could always be found when we were younger. Me and Sienna roll our eyes in unison, a silent truce between us. Nothing permanent, just a small temporary measure to keep mom happy.

'Don't worry about us, mom. I'm more interested to hear how you've been holding up while I've been away.' I ask, quick to change the subject, eager to take the heat away from me and Sienna, while also needing to hear that she's been alright while I've been off doing my own thing.

'Oh, you know how it is. I've been plodding along as best I can.' A small smile creeps onto her lips but this time it doesn't meet her eyes. A sure sign that something is off. My mom's keeping something from me, and I don't like it—not one little bit.

'You sure?' I question while raising a suspicious brow at Sienna. 'What are you two keeping from me?'

My mom's hand falls and rests on my shoulder, before giving me a reassuring squeeze. 'Nothing you need to worry yourself with, son.' She lowers a plate of bacon and eggs down on the table, but my raging appetite instantly vanishes.

'One of you needs to start talking.' I growl out. What the fuck are they keeping from me? My thoughts quickly intensify and go on overdrive.

Is mom sick? Fuck. I shift in my seat as a deep sense of unease ripples deep in my gut, making me feel nauseous.

'It's just weird, is all'. Mom confirms, her voice strong and steady as she lowers herself down in the seat next to me. 'Everything is changing so fast. It gets lonely around here sometimes, what with you being away and Sienna off doing her own thing.' A sharp stab of guilt pierces my chest once more, reminding me just how selfish and self-centered my actions are, and I feel like the world's worst son.

I should have been here. Does mom need me around more than she's willing to acknowledge?

Fuck... fuck... fuck. How could I have been so blind to miss this? My fists clench under the table, my unruly emotions ebbing and flowing like an unstable volcano deep inside me, threatening to erupt at any moment.

I knew I should have been here. I should have made more of an effort to come back home. To check on my mom from time to time. Hell, even the odd phone call here and there wouldn't have been too much trouble.

Deep down I already know this, but sometimes... scrap that, most of the time, my selfish side takes over. It's unintentional, and to be fair I don't even realize it's happening—not until it's too late and the irreversible damage has already been done.

Running a weary hand along my stubbled jaw, I silently acknowledge that I need to try harder—much harder. I need to be so much better when it comes to checking in and stopping by to see my mom. On the only person who has stepped up for me. Who has been there for me over the years—through thick or thin; bad or good... rain or fucking shine.

The only person on the face of this earth who actually gives a damn about what happens to me.

'And...' she says, pulling me out of my thoughts. 'It's only going get lonelier around here soon...'

I snap my eyes toward her, the unease growing more intense with each second that passes. She's sick... I fucking know it. My brows knit together, instant denial setting in. 'What do you mean?' I almost choke on the emotion in my voice, and I struggle to clear my throat.

My mom places her small hand on mine and my heart stops, free falling straight to my stomach, my blood running cold. This is it... the moment I've spent a lifetime dreading. The demons in the back of my mind telling me that she'll leave me eventually, just-like everyone else. How am I supposed to sit here and listen to this bullshit? I refuse to believe that my mom is indestructible.

Before I get a chance to move, her hand clamps around mine, squeezing hard and I'm forced to look at her, straight into her warm brown eyes. I'm surprised, completely taken back when I don't see my own fear looking back at me. There's no pain and sorrow, and instead she smiles and a flicker of pride flashes to life on her face. 'Hasn't Sienna told you?'

'Told me what?' I demand, my head doing a complete three hundred and sixty.

A small rumble of laughter fills the stagnant air between us as my mom finally breaks the dreaded silence and says... 'She'll be joining you at Greenmount. She leaves tomorrow.'

Are you being for real right now? 'How... why... ' I stammer, struggling to form the words which desperately want to come out, but I end up backtracking. This cannot be happening. Greenmount is my escape and the last thing I need in my life is my bitchy ass spoiled brat of a baby sister following me around campus.

Greenmount is the one place I can truly be myself without having to worry about being judged. Without having to worry about the demons of my past coming to the surface. How the hell am I supposed to do that with Sienna hanging off my back and breathing down my neck all the goddamn time?

'Wait...' Sienna flashes her icy blue eyes toward me, her own victorious smile playing on her lips. 'Didn't I tell you?'

'Like fuck you did.' I grind out through my teeth, suddenly unable to keep hold of my composure. This is a step too fucking far and she sure as hell knows it too. I bet she's loving every single second of this.

'Well, maybe if you came home once in a while, I would have been able to share my epic life changing news with you.'

'It's the best news, isn't it?' Mom smiles. 'My babies back together again.'

I inwardly groan, struggling to match my mom's enthusiasm. I haven't seen my mom look this happy in so long, and I know I should be happy too, but truthfully, I can't think of anything worse. This right here is my worst fucking nightmare. A nightmare which is fast becoming my new reality.

'Let's eat.' Mom reaches across the table, indicating the food she's just made, like she usually would, like my whole world hasn't just been turned upside down and shattered. 'I sure hope you're hungry because it doesn't matter what you tell me, Jett... Your momma knows those people don't feed you right while you're away.'

'Oh, come on, mom. Let's be real for a moment. Jett isn't going to turn down food.' Sienna snarls, her disgust still evident on her face. 'Rumor has it, Jett isn't the type of guy to turn down most things.' Her eyes flash to mine and I hear her hidden message loud and clear. *'Except me.'* If she's hunting for an apology, then she's going to be waiting for a lifetime because she isn't about to get one. Not now... not tomorrow, and the future isn't looking all too hopeful either. I'm not apologizing for not fucking her. No fucking way.

If that makes me a hard-faced bastard, then so be it. I have morals, granted not many, but morals all the same.

I really wish I didn't know what her problem is, but I do. I don't get to play ignorant in this situation, but there is one small silver lining—this is her problem to deal with—not mine. I'm sure I'll have to remind myself of that a fair few times. I'm also quick to remind myself that today isn't about mine and Sienna's issues. No, today is about mom. I have all the time in the world to deal with Sienna's bullshit, especially now she's going to be everywhere I turn. Right now, I'm home, checking in with mom before another chaotic semester begins.

I came home to relax. To have some much-needed downtime, before the mask slips back into place and I'm forced to put on my never-ending act for all to see.

Home is the one true place where I get a chance to unwind... to really assess my life. I'll never openly admit it, but this is the only place I can truly hide away from all the glory of my Captain status. From the never-ending attention and all too time-consuming puck bunnies—something else which I'm not willing to allow Sienna to ruin for me.

I guess I best make the most of my limited freedom. My last few hours of peace because from tomorrow, campus is about to turn into the mother of all nightmares.

Why, oh, why did Sienna have to go and choose Greenmount? She could have easily stayed here and enrolled at Ravendale. But then I guess that wouldn't have been much fun for her. Sienna has never been all to attracted to the simple life.

Pissing me off and getting deep under my skin is more her style and specialty. Well, it sure looks like its mission accomplished to me.

Biting down, I swallow hard against the bitter taste in my mouth, forcing myself to smile at my mom as I feign a mixture of happiness and pride. It's not much of a challenge. I've always been a pro when it comes to wearing my famous poker face. But make no mistake, I'll be having it out with Sienna the second mom is out of earshot. If she wants to play games with me then she's gonna be in for a real treat. Games are what I play best.

No way am I going to stand back and watch as she tries to come and ruin everything I've built for myself at Greenmount. I've worked way too hard, busted my balls, both through work and pleasure to get to where I am, and it will take more than a jumped up jealous butch to come along and ruin it all for me.

Sister or not, if she tries to fuck with me and my plans then she'll pay just like the rest of them. No second chances. No mercy.

'Let him eat.' My mom cuts into my thoughts some more. 'He's a growing boy.' She doesn't say anything else, feeling no need to elaborate and obviously sensing the tension simmering between us, which keeps growing thicker and heavier around us. For whatever reason, mom has decided against calling us out like she usually would, and a small part of me is relieved.

'Let's hope golden boy doesn't choke then.' Sienna hisses back, and I laugh sadistically which I know will only piss her off some more. Sienna will never be able to get one over on me.

'Keep wishing, biscuit.'

'Anyway...' Sienna quickly changes the subject when she realizes she isn't about to get a rise out of me, her psychotic split personality coming front and center—a whole new persona creeping onto her small, delicate face. 'Seeing how you're back home, you should come to the party down at the Lake tonight. Unless you're too cool for us kids now?'

I shake my head and laugh, all grievances temporarily forgotten. 'If there's a party happening then I'll be there.' It wouldn't be a party without my name on the list and Sienna knows it too. Plus, there's bound to be plenty of first year's hanging around too. No doubt lost and desperate to fit in with the popular crowd. They'll be desperate to find their feet in Greenmount, and who better to offer them a little helping hand; a push in the right direction than yours truly.

My eyes light up when I think about the endless amount of pussy which will be lapping up my dick tonight. Sienna might be my new *permanent* headache, but I guess she's not all bad. She still has her uses from time to time.

CHAPTER SIX
MILA

'It's party time.'

I find Skye leaning against my truck as I walk out of my mom's rundown apartment and breathe a sigh of relief. Fortunately, I haven't had any run ins with her as she's still comatose following her binge last night and I'm not stupid enough to disturb her. No doubt she'll be straight on the phone to me when she finally resurfaces back into the land of the living, demanding this and that from me. Until that dreaded time comes, I've decided to break free of her wicked restraints, ready to see what's so great about some stupid lame ass beach party.

If the decision was down to me and if I wasn't such a people pleaser I'd probably give it a miss, but seeing how I'm the one who's feeling guilty for being the bad guy as I'm ditching my best friend, completely leaving her behind as she likes to make out, it makes sense for me to pacify her—to do this one last thing for her—kind of like a goodbye gift.

I just hope I don't live to regret my decision.

'What's with the long face?' She demands. 'Aren't you excited?'

'Sure,' I reply. 'This party is what I've been living for.' The sarcasm falls heavily from my tongue and I don't even feel bad about it.

'Oh, come on, Mila... you'll have a total blast when you get there. Trust me.' Thats the problem, I don't trust any of Skye's so-called epic plans because they always end in disaster, and if I'm being honest, I can't see this one turning out any differently.

'I'm already pumped.' I lie, failing to sound as enthusiastic as I'd initially hoped.

'Yeah... okay... maybe you should try telling your face that before we get there.' She narrows her eyes, clearly annoyed that I'm not in the party spirit, and I can feel the disappointment oozing out of her every pore. 'You look like you've just been slapped across the face with a dead fish and forced to eat its eyeballs.'

I can't help but crack a genuine smile and laugh at her ridiculous comment. Skye has always been a little extra and I really can't see that changing any time soon, not that I'd ever want it to.

'Fine... I'll admit, I'm not stoked about going, but I'm also pretty curious to see what the big fuss is all about.' I widen my eyes at my best friend as if to say, *'happy now?'* before I open my truck door and climb inside. 'You of all people should know that parties aren't really my idea of a good time.'

Skye knows I don't have the best relationship with alcohol, what with my mom abusing it so much over the years. Whenever I'm in a crowded place and someone has had a little too much to drink, it automatically triggers some kind of traumatic response in me. My anxiety kicks in, my inner child running scared, my brain automatically programmed to think of the worst-case scenario. I always end up frozen, rooted to the spot, riddled with fear as it cripples my mind and body.

It sounds hella crazy, but my mom's addiction issues are one of the main reasons I don't want to leave Frankie's. I know I could hands down get bar work anywhere, especially near campus, but that's a headache I have no plans of taking on. Especially if I don't have anyone around on hand to help me out, to put my mind at ease. It's just another disaster waiting to happen.

'Just know that I'm doing this for you and only you.' I remind Skye firmly as she jumps into the passenger side, her killer six-inch heels almost scratching my dash as she stretches her endless legs before rewarding me with a gleeful smile.

'I know.' She pulls the visor down and touches up her lip gloss, 'and you're the best friend in the whole wide world. I'm just hoping there's some hot guys there.'

Of course, she is. Skye doesn't do anything without some kind of hidden agenda. Shaking my head, I allow my honey blonde hair to fall into my face, conveniently hiding my smile. All Skye ever thinks about is hot guys. They're the first thing she thinks about when she wakes up, spends all day daydreaming about them, then they're the last thing on her mind before she goes to sleep at night. She's obsessed.

'Well, I hate to break it to you but you didn't have me convinced you were going for the freshmen experience.' More sarcasm drips from my mouth which in turn grants me one of Skye's death glares. One which could kill instantly.

'Don't knock it until you've tried it.' She bites back before turning her attention to her make-up. 'You never know, you could meet the love of your life; your soul mate at this party tonight.'

'Hmm... Somehow I doubt that very much, Skye.'

'Oh my god,' she squeals, snapping her head to the side so she can get a good look at me. 'You're not over Cole, are you?'

'No'. I respond without hesitation, surprising myself in the process, and neither of us miss the defensiveness in my tone. But it's true. I'm not hung up on him, I just really don't want to talk about him. Cole has finally shown his true colors and I don't particularly like them all too much, but that also doesn't mean I can just forget about him. *About us*. I can't just move on with some random guy. A meaningless fling isn't really my style. Plus, we haven't exactly broken up. Neither one of us has said the words or made it official. Cole just walked away from me and I haven't heard from him since.

In my mind, we're over. I am so done with his drama, but Skye must be crazy if she thinks I'm going to this party just to hook up with some random stranger. That might be her style, and I've never been one to judge. Each to their own and all that, but it's just not for me at all.

'You don't sound too sure about that.'

'Oh, believe me,' I bite back, forcing the conviction into my voice, 'I'm one hundred percent sure, but Cole is the least of my problems right now.' I reluctantly allow my mind to float back to my mom, and my heart starts to race. I shouldn't be worrying about her. She's no longer my problem but no matter how hard I try to forget her, to force her to the back of my mind. she's always there, front and center—niggling away, reminding me that she'll be straight on my case when she finally comes around from her alcohol induced coma.

I quickly decide I can't be dealing with that kind of drama right now. Not tonight, and without so much as another thought I pull my phone out of my bag and turn it off. My mom won't be able to hound me now.

Tomorrow I'll be leaving Coldwater. Only one more night to get through and I'll finally be free. Free of all previous responsibilities. I mean, what's the worst that can happen in one night?

Skye side eyes me from the passenger before I toss my phone back into my bag. 'Do you want to talk about it?'

'Nope.' I emphasize the P so she knows to drop the subject and when she looks away, I buckle up and start the engine.

―――

Thirty minutes later were pulling into Greenmount Grove, a small lake situated at the end of town, and even though it's not all too far away from Coldwater, I still feel like I've been transported to a completely different universe.

Where Coldwater is all grey, murky and miserable, Greenmount is a haven surrounded by trees and endless greenery. It's almost as though I've somehow manifested the mystical forest of my daydreams into my reality. From the never-ending foliage surrounding us, straight down to the vast ocean, glistening in the moonlight, it's waves calmly crashing behind the mountains in the distance.

I open my mouth in awe as I try to take it all in, imprinting the beauty before me, memorizing the vast mixture of jades, emeralds and deep greens. 'Wow...' is all I manage to say.

'This place is something else, right? 'Skye says beside me.

'No shit. I didn't realize this place would turn out to be so breathtaking.' It's no secret that I've never stepped outside of Coldwater and I wrongly judged this place. I automatically assumed every town in our state was hidden under the very same rainclouds of doom—but I couldn't have been any further from the truth. I couldn't have been any more wrong.

'So, this is how the other half live, huh?' Skye whistles while taking in the epic sight before us.

'I swear this is just like the magical forest I dream up in my fantasies...' in my gloriously deluded daydreams. A small laugh escapes me when a thought comes into my mind and slowly clicks into place. How could I have been so stupid? Obviously, this must be where the name Greenmount comes from.

'This is going to be so much fun.' Skye is quick to pull her feet down from the dash before gleefully rubbing her hands together and I can see she's finding it hard to contain her excitement. Once again, a part of me wishes I could find it within me to share her enthusiasm.

For me, the fun won't begin until I start my new life: My next chapter. Tomorrow. This little adventure tonight is purely for Skye's benefit and her benefit alone. A treasured memory she can always come back to when she's feeling down, lost or lonely while I'm the one who'll be out here too busy to enjoy it while studying my ass off.

'All right... how about we get this over with?' I sigh dramatically as I kill the engine, fast realizing there's no going back now. We're well and truly past the point of no return.

I climb out of my truck and my anxiety kicks in. A dark cloud instantly blanketing me. Straight away my intuition is telling me that I'm not going to fit in here. I'm going to be so out of place, sticking out like a sore thumb. Everyone will take one look at me and see I'm from out of town, and right now I have no idea if that's a good or a bad thing.

All I know is nobody likes an outcast. But surely, I can't be the only one who's going to be travelling to Greenmount from a distance. There must be heaps of people who have travelled further than me.

Skye jumps out of the truck and spins around on her killer heels, slowly taking it all in. 'Mila, look at this place.'

I cast my eyes around and they fall on a narrow dirt path which I'm guessing leads right down to the lake. Just behind the trees a mass of fairy lights twinkle in the distance, some lighter ones glowing along the dirt path helping people find their way. It looks like the party has already started, no doubt overly crowded, bursting at the seams with excited kids who are also finding their freedom. Eager to find their way in this crazy life.

'I can't do this, Skye.' I confess, my voice as soft as a whisper. What was I thinking? I'm well and truly out of my comfort zone here. I'm overwhelmed. All I want to do is climb back inside my truck and get the hell out of here.

My social anxiety is through the roof and I haven't even made it down to the main event yet. 'Do we really need to be here?' I ask, hoping she'll hear the pain in my voice and say we can forget about it and leave. But this is Skye we're talking about. She's the type of girl who's up for anything—and I mean anything.

'Hey,' she reaches out and takes my cold, clammy hand. 'Breathe. I promise you'll be fine. You'll feel more relaxed and at ease once you've started to mingle.'

Another wild rush of anxiety shudders through me at her words. 'But I don't want to mingle.' The last thing I want to do is mingle. I guess I should have expected this kind of response, especially since Skye always has boys on the brain.

'Mila, I've told you...' She waggles her flawless brows at me, 'The best way to get over a guy is to slide straight under the next one. One day you'll start listening to me and you'll soon see my logic is the way forward.'

I don't even bother to acknowledge her stupidity with a dignified response. We've been here many times before and it will end up in some crazy heated debate. A debate I don't have the time or energy for. Instead, I inhale a deep lungful of salty air and I use everything I have to clear my mind before linking my arm in Skye's.

'Let's get this shit show on the road.' I bite out reluctantly, and my best friend beams back at me, her eyes glistening with excitement as she leads me down the narrow dirt path, straight into no doubt the worst mistake of my life.

'Thats my girl.' She laughs encouragingly before pulling me closer to her. I allow her to take the lead as our feet move down the sandy path and when we come to the end of the dirt path my mouth falls open in shock. 'Shit... I wasn't expecting this.' I admit out loud, my eyes growing wide as I take in the epic sight before me. Totally speechless and mesmerized by the endless amount of flashing lights twinkling around me.

'What did you expect?' Skye laughs beside me. 'You only head back to campus once every year.' She shakes her head at me like I'm the one who's just grown two heads.

'I don't know. They don't do things like this at Ravendale.'

'That's because Ravendale has nothing on this place, baby.'

'True.' I confess, still looking around quickly. At least this whole set up is out of the way, hidden behind endless trees. 'I just didn't expect the whole Lake to be turned into some wild fun fair.'

'Greenmount obviously pulls out all the stops, and I for one am not about to start complaining. Now come on, if we stand around here all night, we'll end up missing all the fun.

CHAPTER SEVEN
MILA

The wind picks up and sweeps across my face and through my hair as I listen to the rhythmic waves crashing against the mountains and I'm surprised to find it soothing my soul... cleaning my mind and filtering out the masses around me, an unusual sense of calm flowing through me in such a chaotic place.

The clouds roll in, another storm brewing as the wind picks up speed, sweeping around us. So much for wondering if the weather is any different in Greenmount compared to Coldwater.

It didn't take Skye all too long to leave me high and dry. She was desperate to walk around, check out the mini stalls and mingle, and I was more than happy for her to do her own thing. She asked me to go with her but the thought of losing myself in the masses filled me with dread. No way would I willingly get all close and personal with so many crowded bodies.

I'll play along for Skye's sake, but I'll do it hidden away in the shadows. In a safe space where no one will bother me.

I looked around and quickly found a vacant wooden log by the fire pit—the perfect place to keep myself to myself.

The fire pit was empty, so it seemed like the perfect place to take my sorry ass, hoping to hide away and lose myself in a little piece and quiet until Skye decided to call it a night. God knows how long it will take her to get her fill.

Like most things in life, the peace didn't last all too long and before I had chance to get comfortable, a dark silhouette graced my peripheral, and casually claimed the space next to me. Maybe the right thing for me to do would be to glance sideways and offer them a small smile, to say hello, but my social anxiety kicks in, forcing me to keep my eyes forward, completely captivated by the flames as they ripple and flicker in the wind.

'You don't like people much, do you?' A small female voice asks, and she sounds friendly enough.

'Is it that obvious? 'The words leave my lips before I have a chance to stop them, shocking myself in the process. I don't usually talk to strangers If I'm by myself, yet here I am doing the unthinkable.

'You bet. So, what's your story?'

'My story?' Confusion sweeps across my face. Why would this girl want to know my story?

'Are you starting at Greenmount or are you already there?' Her comment piques my interest. I'm guessing this girl is first year too. She sounds unsure about my position at Greenmount.

I slowly turn my head to look at her. 'First year.' I answer and I'm met with a pair of piercing blue eyes and a friendly smile, slowly ebbing away my crippling anxiety.

'Same, but girl let me tell you something...' her smile grows wider, almost like she's about to let me in on some hidden secret. 'You're gonna have to snap out of this shy girl persona you've got going on when you start.'

'I'm not following.' I confess, not sure whether I should be relieved someone wants to help me out or offended that she's assuming I'm an empty shell.

'Look,' she rubs her hands together before warming them by the fire. 'Greenmount is a big place, but don't be fooled. Believe me when I tell you that everyone knows everyone.'

'That's cool, and I appreciate the heads up but I'm more than happy to keep myself to myself.'

Another laugh flutters through the air between us. 'Oh girl, you're in for the shock of your life.'

'Hang on, if this is your first year too, then how do you know so much?' I question, my curiosity getting the better of me.

Her blue eyes watch me, taking me in some more as she tries to get a read on me before rocking her shoulder against mine. 'I think we'll be good friends, you and me. But a little advice, ask no questions and be told no lies.'

Great. Now this strange chick has decided to talk to me in riddles. Where the hell is Skye and what's taking her so long? I swear, she better not have hooked up with some random guy. If she's forgotten all about me then I'll have no choice but to fend for myself.

Okay, I'll admit, I might have been stupid enough to agree to come here, purely so she could have some fun, but I sure as hell didn't sign up to be abandoned. To be left out in the dark.

'I'm Sienna by the way.' I look at the girl next to me and decide maybe I could actually use a friend, or more importantly, an associate who'd be able to show me around when I arrive on campus tomorrow. Sienna seems to know what she's talking about, and she could eventually become a much-needed ally.

'Mila. 'I nod back at her.

'Nice to meet you.' She reaches deep inside her bag and pulls out a beer, holding it out to me. I quickly shake my head, politely declining her offer. Another automatic trauma response from living and growing up with an alcoholic in my life. I'm not your average teenager. Alcohol doesn't have the same appeal to me the way it does with everyone else, and that's perfectly okay with me.

I've been programmed from a young age, ensuring I always keep a clear and level head—at all times. I never know how one night is going to play out from one night to the next.

'Not a fan of partying either?' She inquires and I suddenly feel small in the shadow of her judgment.

'Something like that.' I mumble, not ready to go into detail about my messed-up life to a total stranger.

'No worries. I guess it means more for me.' She pulls the cap off and brings the bottle to her lips, a small confident smile curving at the edges. 'So, tell me quiet one, have you travelled far?'

Probably not, but for what it's worth this is the first time I've left my hometown, which is a massive feat for me. I don't need to tell her the whole ins and outs of my life so I simply add, 'Coldwater.' I rub my hands together in front of the campfire, more to keep my mind busy. 'How about you?'

'Greenmount born and bred, baby.' is all Sienna manages to say before another shadow casts over the fire, shrinking us both into darkness.

'Hey dickweed... you got a beer in there for me?' A deep voice booms out around us, and a rush of goose pimples break out across my skin, and I already know they have nothing to do with the arctic air swirling around us.

To my surprise, Sienna snaps her head up and glares at the beast of a guy who's now standing before us, his presence oozing dominance. My gut is warning me to be careful, telling me that whoever this dark shadow of a stranger is, he's bad news and is no friend of Sienna's. My observation is quickly confirmed as a solid fact when she narrows her eyes in disgust.

'Go fuck yourself.' She bites out and I don't miss the bitter venom in her voice.

'Don't be like that, Cee.' He growls back, his tone just as bitter. He steps closer to the fire, his angular face still cast in a deep shadow but his piercing jade green eyes lock onto mine and shoot an arrow of ice through my already erratically damaged heart. 'We're all friends here, right?'

'Are you deaf as well as stupid? I said go... fuck... yourself...' she punctuates each word so he'll hopefully understand her better and I have to admit, this girl—whoever she is, she's sure packing some mighty big balls standing up to him like that.

He ignores her, clearly used to her reaction and continues like she hasn't even spoken. 'Talking of friends...' I see a small smirk dancing in the flames. 'Don't be rude, Cee. Why don't you introduce me to your new friend here?'

'Wait... are we suddenly cool enough to be seen talking to the great Jett Jameson now?'

An evil, sinister glint flickers in the stranger's eyes and it's pretty obvious to me that there's no love lost between these two. The air around us is sizzling with a heated distaste, growing heavier by the second and I'd be lying if I said I didn't feel uncomfortable.

This dark and brooding creature decides to ignore Sienna again, proving she's no threat to him and his intentions suddenly focus elsewhere... *on me*.

The silence grows thick and heavy with nothing but the sound of crashing waves somewhere in the distance.

My rapid, uneven heartbeat pounds loudly deep inside my ears as his large muscular frame slowly moves around the fire pit—a seasoned predator stalking his prey. Danger and destruction ooze out of his every pore, his whole aura buzzing in warning.

This boy is no good.

He's bad news.

Evil to the core.

My mind is screaming at me to stay away from him. To get up and run. To run and never look back, but my body chooses this moment to betray me and my screaming subconscience. I'm frozen in place. I'm rooted to the spot with no means of a way out. I'm trapped, held captive by his hungry jade green eyes, and he knows it too.

As if my body couldn't betray me anymore, my breathing hitches, catching in my throat when he moves even closer... all of his attention focused solely on me.

I don't like it.

A multitude of foreign emotions flood my body from just one look and the heat prickling my skin has nothing to do with the blazing flames from the fire in front of me. No... the heat, the intense unbearable heat is radiating from this tall, dark and dangerous creature moving toward me.

'What's your name?' He asks, his hypnotic voice as smooth as butter and I hear a low chuckle coming from his friend somewhere behind him. I'm affected and everyone can see it. I shrink in on myself, an automatic response. A reaction he doesn't miss. 'Don't be shy. Ignore the Queen of doom beside you. We're all friends here.' He crouches down so he can face me at eye level and his gigantic frame completely dwarfs me into the shadow of his glorious importance.

I don't know him, but he oozes authority. If I had to guess I'd place all bets that this is the guy who calls all the shots around here.

'For the third and final time, go fuck yourself Jett.' Sienna bites out, but her words don't break our connection. 'You're not welcome here.'

'Says who, you?' Another wicked smirk dances onto his lips, a small dimple appearing on his right cheek... and he doesn't take his eyes off mine.

Fuck, I'm melting just looking at him. A useless puddle at his feet.

'Yeah, says me.' I'll admit, this girl isn't afraid to hold her own around this guy. Hell, he intimidates me just by looking at him. 'Why don't you go and find some other first year's to annoy.'

He leans closer. leaning to my right, his knee grazing mine, shooting a sharp jolt of electricity through my body, the static pulsating as he darts his eyes toward Sienna. 'I wasn't talking to you so how about you do yourself a favor and keep that smart ass mouth of yours shut for once...'

Silence sizzles in the air between us. Sienna and Jett glare at each other, each refusing to back down. His brows furrow, a stark warning... a look I've witnessed many times before. 'Ignore her.' His angular face, all sharp cheek bones and edges instantly changes when he turns his attention back to me again, his perfect dimple coming out to play once more. 'Sienna gets a little shitty when the attention isn't focused on her. I wouldn't take it personally if I were you.'

Jett instantly disarms me with another killer smile, leaving me vulnerable and exposed to his deadly charms. I'm rendered speechless as his midnight black hair falls down into his eyes and when he looks at me through his dark lashes; dark lashes which frame his magnetic eyes, my body instantly responds to him. My heart skyrockets, pounding hard in my chest and my palms are slick with sweat.

What the hell is this guy doing to me? 'What's your name, princess?' He asks again, bringing his devilish face closer to mine, so close that his nose is almost flush with my own, and all train of thought leaves my mind.

'Mila....' I stammer on a whisper, the words freely falling from my mouth before I have a chance to stop them. This dark and brooding Adonis seems to have some crazy kind of hold over me—a hold I can't pull away from, no matter how hard I try.

His Adams apple bobs slightly, his own eyebrows raising knowingly as he watches me swallow down hard on the solid lump which has formed at the back of my throat. Jett knows he has me where he wants me and much to my surprise, he chooses this moment—a stupid and reckless moment of weakness, to press his warm lips against mine.

I don't move straight away. I'm too shocked to move. I'm too shocked to breathe. All I can do is remain still as the heat of his soft lips burn my mouth, but not in a bad way. His manly scent, mixed with a crisp touch of Cedarwood and sea salt invades my senses, consuming every fiber of my being.

'What the fuck do you think you're playing at?' I vaguely hear Sienna's voice calling out from somewhere in the distance. 'Get off her, you dick.' She snaps louder this time and I feel the smooth curve of his mouth on my lips, a low chuckle building deep in his chest before I finally snap out of my Jett induced trance and pull my head back, away from him, my mouth open and my eyes wide with shock.

I'll be honest, with the heat of this strangers lips no longer on mine, I feel cold. Empty, and a wild rush of confusion sweeps through my body. If I'm being completely truthful, I don't know whether to be relieved or secretly disappointed that I've been brought straight back down to reality.

Quickly deciding I can't take the heat anymore, the suspense and crippling anxiety that this dark and dangerous creature seems to bring out in me, not to mention the multitude of foreign emotions he's managed to somehow evoke from deep within me. I think it's probably in my best interests to get out of here while I still can and put some much-needed distance between us before something stupid and reckless happens. Something I know I'll live to regret.

If I don't see this guy again for the rest of my life it still won't be long enough. All I can do is hope and pray that our paths don't cross again.

Without thinking about it further. I use everything I have and push myself up from the wooden log, desperate to get away from this unfamiliar situation and find Skye so we can get the hell out of here, and I have every intention of putting tonight's events behind me, happily pretending they didn't happen.

'It was nice meeting you, Sienna.' I say as I offer her a weak smile, trying my hardest to be polite. She seems nice enough, and I'd hate to offend her. Maybe I'll see her around campus from time to time, but right now I need to get out of here and fast.

I need to breathe.

I need to clear my head.

I need to find Skye before I forget who I am and what I'm doing here. Before I lose all forms of composure.

CHAPTER EIGHT

JETT

'Do you wanna tell me what the fuck that was about?' I demand, my chest rising and falling with the heat of my anger as it bubbles deep within me and rushes to the surface.

'I don't need to explain myself to you.' Sienna hisses back and her blue eyes are ablaze with a mixture of pure hatred and disgust. Well, the feelings fucking mutual.

'That's where you're wrong, my darling baby sister.'

'Don't patronize me.'

'Who's patronizing? Not me. I'm just laying down some facts. You see, if you're big enough to come and play on my patch, then damn straight you'll explain yourself to me. Greenmount is my territory. It's my playground. In case you're not following, that means I make the rules around here and everyone else follows.'

'Seriously, Jett, have you actually heard yourself?' She growls back. 'Who do you think you are? Some kind of God.'

I flash her another smile which only makes her scrunch her face some more. 'All you have to do is ask around and every person in this town will validate that yes, I am God. Nothing, including your unwelcome appearance will ever change that. Not you or your smart-ass mouth. I'm the hero here, and if you don't like it then maybe you should run back to mom's and enroll somewhere else. Somewhere more suited like, I don't know... Ravendale.'

'Anyone ever tell you you're a waste of spunk?'

'Daily.' I Laugh. 'What's your point?' Sienna of all people should know I couldn't give a damn when it comes to other people's opinions, especially If their opinions are of me.

'My point is... you just jumped all over that new girl. Like you could...'

'Again... your point...' I fake a yawn so she can tell this conversation is boring the crap out of me. She shakes her head at me, her mouth open, eyes wide with disbelief.

'Didn't you see how uncomfortable she was? She was absolutely petrified, and it was embarrassing as fuck, Jett.'

'Uncomfortable my ass.' Anyone could see that girl was desperate for me, the same way every other girl in this town is. 'What's wrong, Cee... what's this really about? Can't deal with me making a move on the new girls?'

She shakes her head before pulling herself up to her full five-foot five height and it's laughable. Against me she looks tiny—like an ant. One I could squish in a nano-second, but for some fucked-up reason, a reason I don't really know, I always decide to keep her around. 'Not every girl wants to jump on your dick.' The venom is like acid on her tongue.

There's so much I could say in response to her stupid outburst. A pointless reaction to something so irrelevant to her. 'Thats where you're wrong. Green doesn't suit you, Cee.' I laugh and I hear Bennett laughing behind me too as she flares her nostrils in disgust. 'If you're easily offended, Greenmount isn't going to be for you.'

'Are you finished?' She questions, still refusing to back down.

'Not yet. What are you doing here anyways? I thought you'd be bored already.' Sienna takes me in some more as she finally lowers herself back down on the wooden log, casually opening another beer.

'I'm a first year remember. This party is for me, not you.' How could I forget? It's all she's been harping on about all day. 'I have every right to be here,' pulling the beer to her lips, I watch as she takes a long draw. 'I guess I should be asking you the same question. I mean, aren't you a little past your sell by? I thought you'd be over there trying to hang out with the newbies.'

I can't fight the laugh which consumes me as I look down at my little sister. 'I'll never be past my sell by. The chicks in this town love me. They'll do anything and I mean anything to get close to me. I know it. You know it. The whole of Greenmount knows it. Nothing and no one will be able to change that, and that girl you're so worried about, you can bet your ass she'll be fantasizing about me in her dreams tonight...' My voice oozes confidence and I know Sienna hates it with a passion.

Like I said, I was born to win at this thing we call life. This is my fate and there's not all too much I can do about it, except lap it up and enjoy every moment.

The music pulsates in my ears as I wander through the mass of bodies taking over the lake. Endless first years and heaps of puck bunnies who I've already fucked; with zero intention of going back for seconds. One rodeo is all they get on this racehorse, so they need to make sure they enjoy it while it lasts.

The crowds quickly disperse when they notice my presence. It's always biblical, like Moses parting the red sea, and to be fair I'm not hard to miss. Even the newbies notice me, automatically sensing I'm someone of importance. Someone of a much higher ranking than them, and they watch me, eyes wide, their mouths almost touching the floor.

I don't stop to take in the epic sight before me. Not like I usually would. Instead, I cast my eyes lazily around the dancing bodies, but my mind is on overdrive. Dead set on its mission. Already focused elsewhere... my attention solely fixed on one person...

Mila...

I'm sure that's what she said she was called. But her name's not important. It's totally irrelevant. All I know is I need to find her, and fast.

Never once in all my years, the years I've spent dominating this town, has a girl ever thought about, let alone dared to walk away from me. Her stormy hazel eyes flash in my mind haunting me, and a mixture of strange, totally foreign emotions ripple deep in my chest. I don't know what's happening, but from the moment our eyes connected, she's somehow managed to bury herself deep in my mind and under my skin—like a persistent itch I can't seem to scratch.

I think it's high time she learned her first lesson in Greenmount.

A lesson in learning exactly who I am, and I'm more than happy to give it to her. To hand deliver it personally... if only I could find her again.

'Yo, dude... wait up.' I hear Bennett calling out from behind me, struggling to keep up with my urgent strides. 'Where's the fire?' He laughs with an undercurrent of uncertainty. Bennett isn't used to this kind of reaction from me. He's well and truly in the dark. Bennett doesn't realize, not even for a second how serious this situation is.

'The fire?' I call back. 'The fire fucking blazed and exploded the second that smart-ass bitch upped and walked away from me.' Straight out of my line of sight like she never fucking existed. Like I'm a fucking no body.

'Who?' I turn my head to look at Bennett and watch as his brows furrow in confusion. 'That chick by the Lake with Sienna?'

'The very one.' I bite back, unintentionally taking my frustration out on him. 'I need to find her.'

'Hold up...' Bennett quickly comes up in front of me, causing me to falter in my tracks. Not what I need right now.

'Move out of my way, bro.' I warn. I don't have time for his games, yet he still stands tall, showing no signs of moving, and the sadistic son of a bitch actually has the audacity to laugh in my face.

'Shit. Are my eyes deceiving me or is Jett Jameson actually running around after some random chick?' He whistles through his teeth before running a casual hand through his blond curls. 'Just when I thought I'd seen and heard it all, the master of disguise goes and surprises me again.'

I narrow my eyes and glare at him, silently warning him that this isn't the time or the place. Warning him to keep below his station and to step very fucking carefully.

'I'm not running after anyone.'

'Oh, yeah... sure you're not.' Bennett rolls his eyes, refusing to buy my bullshit.

'I said I'm not running. End of.' I growl, way too defensive and I know Bennett doesn't miss it. 'She needs teaching a lesson is all, and she needs it fast.' I say, more to convince myself of my true motives.

'A lesson?' Obviously, Bennett isn't following protocol.

'Did you see her? Did you see the way the jumped-up little bitch looked at me? Like I was a piece of shit... someone beneath her, and then she had the fucking nerve to get up and walk away from me.'

'Yeah, I caught that.' He runs a weary hand along his jaw, trying and failing to hide a smile. 'But you have to admit she might have been a little taken aback when you planted one on her.'

'Get fucked, man. Everyone knows getting hit on by me is a rite of passage. '

'Even so, I'm guessing that set back can't have been all too good for the ego.' He laughs some more, and I have to stop myself from smacking the smug look from his face.

'This isn't funny, dick face. This is serious. If this gets around Greenmount then my reputation could be fucked, damaged beyond repair.'

'Hate to break it to you man, but it's funny as fuck from where I'm standing.' He pauses for a moment. 'Actually, it's more than funny. Jett Jameson chasing pussy is fucking hilarious. The rest of the guys are gonna think they'll have easy pickings of the new girls if they're willingly walking away from Greenmount's hockey hero...'

I allow his words to sink in, and I'd be lying if I said they didn't sting like a motherfucker. Bennett isn't wrong, but there's no way in hell I'm about to admit that to him.

'Well, I wouldn't be running around after her if Sienna had kept her big mouth shut. She just can't seem to help herself. She always has to go and get caught up in my life, and now I'll have no means of an escape. I'm going to have to deal with her bullshit on the daily. Fuck, my head hurts just thinking about it.'

I round the candy stall, not paying attention to my surroundings, used to the masses of Greenmount instantly parting for me to pass without any hesitation, and crash into a small figure. A figure which moans out in protest, but I'm not about to hang around and apologize. The stupid jerk should have been watching where they were going. At six-foot five, it's not like I'm hard to miss.

'Watch where you're fucking going.' I growl out, my anger and frustration at being humiliated rush to the surface. I'm in no mood to be hanging around. When the figure doesn't move out of my way, I grit my teeth and look down, gracing whatever peasant with my presence. If they won't move, then I'm not afraid to make them move... with my bare hands. If they want to spend their time gawping at me then that's cool, I have no issues with that, but they'll have to come hang out in the stands like everyone else.

'What's your problem?' I demand, annoyed that this jerk is blocking my way and wasting my time. That's when I see her. The smart-ass bitch I've been searching for. All five-foot nothing of pure annoyance and fuckable beauty standing before me. When she looks up, her stormy hazel eyes pierce into mine and my heart skips a beat, before stopping in my chest. It's quick to kick start again when her mouth forms the perfect O. Perfect enough to wrap around my dick—and that they will. It's only a matter of time before her lips are glistening with my cum after I've deep throated and fucked her mouth red raw. This bitch is gonna wish she'd never met me, let alone dared to walk away from me.

Make no mistake. With a little time and perseverance this little pocket rocket will be mine... used, abused and damaged goods and the thought gets me excited.

'You...' she hisses, her small chest rising and falling at a rapid rate, a mixture of fear and excitement no doubt coursing through her veins. 'I thought I'd seen the last of you.' Her small button nose wrinkles in disgust and her reaction does things to me I never fucking expected.

Who is this chick and where the hell did she come from? I have no doubt in my mind that she's been sent to test me.

I step closer and her eyes widen. 'Quit with the games, princess.'

'Quit calling me that. I already told you my name is Mila.'

I'm quick to offer her my award-winning smile. One which usually causes panties to fall to the floor, happy in the knowledge I'm getting some kind of reaction from her. I now have something over her and my whole-body tingles with sweet victory. 'Princess it is...' Thats' a given.

'Fuck you.' She bites back, refusing to bow down like the other girls do. Mila is going to be hard work, that much I can already tell, and thankfully for me, I sure love a challenge.

'Oh, that's what I'm hoping.' I take another step closer, unable to ignore the crazy magnetic pull between us. Her hazel eyes are still blazing with anger. My effortless charms have zero effect on her. My panty-dropping smile does fuck all. Absolutely nada—fucking zilch.

'Full of yourself, much?'

Leaning down, I bring my face closer, my nose almost flush with hers. I keep my expression void of any emotion as I say, 'Princess, when you're king of this town, it comes naturally to be full of yourself. It's all part of the territory, and if you play your cards right, one day soon you might be full of me too.'

Mila shakes her honey blonde waves before trying to move around me, but she fails at the first hurdle. I'm much faster on my feet. Thanks to endless training sessions and hockey matches, my reflexes are on point, and I block her as though she was the opposition in an instant.

'Move out of my way.' She demands, trying her best to stand tall and keep her head high. I don't entertain her with an answer, instead I use this moment to watch her closely, loving how easily I can get her back up and get some kind of reaction out of her.

This is new. Totally new fucking territory for me and I'm not all too sure how I feel about it. Girls, they usually fall at my feet. They'll do all sorts of crazy shit, desperate to capture my attention—but this chick... she doesn't even seem to notice me. Like, at all, and it's really starting to have an effect on me.

I don't like it. Not one fucking bit. I want this girl to notice me. I need her to notice me. The same way I've noticed her.

'Hey man...' Bennett calls out from somewhere behind me, quickly breaking the magical spell and grabbing my attention, slowly pulling my mind out of an unfamiliar haze. 'You heard the girl. She wants to get passed.'

I hear him loud and clear, but I still keep my curious green eyes locked onto the imposter, on the girl before me. 'What if I don't want to let you past?' I question, anticipation tingling my skin as I wait for her response, but I'm left hanging for the first time in my life when it doesn't come. I've rendered her speechless, and her smart-ass mouth won't function.

Jett one —Mila none. Game, Set, fucking match.

'Mila... there you are.' A high-pitched squeak calls out from somewhere behind me, once again breaking our connection. I watch as Mila's eyes finally leave mine and grow wide, lighting up with relief. 'I've been looking for you everywhere. I've called a hundred times, but it keeps going to voicemail.'

Mila's friend comes to an abrupt stop when she realizes Mila isn't alone. She takes me and Bennett in, sizing us up, noticing I've blocked Mila's path.

'Oh, what's this?' she questions, a deep hunger laced in her voice as she looks up and down, like we're not just the snack but the whole fucking meal. The way girl's usually look at us. The way Mila should be looking at me. 'It looks like someone has been busy making friends.' I can't help but laugh at the accusation in her tone.

'I wouldn't go that far.' Mila bites back, her smart-ass mouth back on top form and a wild fury still blazes in her eyes—directed solely at me.

I have no idea who she is, but she for sure doesn't like me. Usually if people don't like me, I can take it because that's their own opinion. It's on them, but the instant dislike I see when she looks at me has me in the mother of all chokeholds. It rubs me up in all the wrong ways.

Maybe it would have been easier for me to have allowed her to leave. No questions asked. Forget this little pocket rocket even existed, but it's well and truly out of my hands. It's too late. The irreversible damage has been done and she'll be burned to my memory, haunting me every minute of every day until I've managed to find out who she is, and what kind of spell she's put on me.

Mila uses the distraction of her friend to her advantage, to make her move and this time I don't try to stop her. Mila doesn't even hesitate as she shoves her small curvaceous frame past me while reaching out and grabbing her friend's arm before walking away from me without uttering another word... and not for the first time.

'What the fuck has gotten into you?' Bennett demands and for the first time in my life I struggle to find an answer. I wish I knew myself. 'You're acting all kinds of wrong, man.'

'I need to know who she is,' Is all I manage. No one and I mean no one willingly walks away from me and gets away with it.

CHAPTER NINE
MILA

Today is the day.

The day I've spent a whole lifetime waiting for. The very one I've been daydreaming about for as long as I can remember. I pinch myself, still refusing to believe that this is actually happening, happening to little old me.

I'm finally doing the unthinkable. I'm packed up and I'm leaving Coldwater. Granted, it might not be permanent for now, but it's a big step in the right direction, for sure.

My new life starts here and the best thing about it is nothing and no one can try to take my new sense of freedom away from me. No one can stop me and my determination for a better life.

I breathe in a deep lungful of air as the sun briefly breaks free from the clouds blanketing it, and it shines brightly down onto my last box by the old wooden red door, almost like a celebration from the God's above, singing out in harmony, thankful I'm doing what I said I would, leaving this deadbeat town, putting it behind me and never looking back.

Reaching down, I pick up the box, light in my arms and toss it straight into the back of my truck, before turning around and stealing one last glance at the tiny apartment I've been forced to call home for the past eighteen years. It's never really been my home though. Just a vicious battle ground for my mom, her endless abuse, and never-ending demons.

Dusting my hands off on my skinny jeans I climb into my truck before taking another deep calming breath, desperate to keep some form of composure.

'So long, mom.' I say to myself. *'No doubt I'll hear from you soon enough.'*

My mom's battles with alcohol and other recreational substances have taken the mother of all tolls on the both of us. I've probably been impacted the most seeing now I'm the sober one during her vicious and endless attacks. Taking hit after hit.

It's no surprise the woman who birthed me isn't standing tall and proud at the door, all set and ecstatic to wave me off into my new life. A small, idiotic part of me, one which never learns, had secretly hoped she'd surprise me. That she'd be awake at least, but once again she's still out cold after another late-night binge last night. I know she's my mom, a reckless and totally irresponsible one for sure, but her demons can't keep being laid at my feet.

She can't keep expecting me to drop everything and rush to her rescue every time she decides to hit the button on herself-destruct mode. As selfish as it sounds, I'm getting older, and I have my own life to lead. My mom might be too far gone, buried deep in the rabbit hole, but I don't have any plans to mess up my one shot at a brighter future.

I got into Greenmount by my own merit. Not my mother's. I didn't get in after receiving years of unconditional love, nurture, and guidance. I'd never be able to rely on her never-ending support. No, I was the one who made it happen—through hard work and sheer determination. I worked my ass off and I'm not about to stand back while she tries to bring me down to her sluggish level, dead set on ruining my future prospects.

I know it's not going to be easy. All I need to do is survive the next four years at Greenmount and I'll be winning. So long as I keep my head down and work hard, I'm more than confident that I'll ace my degree and then the world will be my oyster.

My eyes dart to the rundown apartment through the rear-view mirror and I'm shocked, because leading up to this moment, a small part of me thought I might-feel something; sorrow, maybe even a sense of loss, but all I feel is a deep-rooted sense of relief. Relief that I'm finally getting out of here. Finally, after a lifetime I'm escaping the traumatic clutches of my mom.

I know it won't be that easy though.

I'm not stupid enough to think she'll step back and leave me to my own devices. Life has never been that kind to me so I can't see a reason for that to change now. There's no doubt in my mind that my mom will be calling me from time to time. Not to check in and have a mother/daughter catch up. Not to see how I'm doing, offering a natural maternal response. No, my mom will be calling as soon as she remembers I exist. When she needs something from me, demanding money and God knows what else. Ruthlessly persevering until she eventually wears me down, draining my energy physically and emotionally until I'm forced to pick up the phone just so I can get her off my back for a little while.

I'm always living on hope. I like to be positive, and maybe this time will be different. In the past I used to allow my mom free access to my mind. I gave her permission to get to me, because I knew her behavior would be inevitable anyway. I was the person who had no choice but to go back to her at the end of every day and night—always living in fear, walking on constant eggshells, never knowing what kind of mood I'd find her in.

But things could be different now... now that I have some place else to stay and we're not trapped under the same roof. Now there'll be no pressure for me to try to keep her sweet. I don't need to worry about rocking the boat, because I'm about to set sail and depart on a completely different ocean.

With that beautiful and positive thought in my mind, I shake my head, removing all thoughts of my mom out of my mind and roll the engine, juddering my truck to life.

This is finally happening.

This is my fresh start and I have zero intentions of bringing along the never-ending raincloud of doom along for the ride. It can stay here in Coldwater with my mom, where it belongs.

―――⁂―――

It doesn't take me all too long to drive into Greenmount. It's only a thirty-minute drive down the highway and I'm proud of myself for arriving in one piece and not getting lost along the way.

I have to admit, the feeling of fresh and crisp autumn air rushing through the window, sweeping through my hair was out of this world, cleansing my soul, freeing me from all previous ties and removing any leftover stagnant energy.

I'm ready.

I am so ready for whatever Greenmount has to offer me. I'm more than happy to rise to any challenge which is thrown my way. My mood is good. Really good.

For the first time in what feels like forever I feel happy, calm, relaxed and full of energy, and I'm not going to allow anyone to burst my little bubble of happiness. I have every intention of staying perched on my fluffy cloud for the rest of my living days.

I'm shocked by how quiet Greenmount is compared to Coldwater when I hit a right and drive into my new hometown, and once again my vision is filled with endless greenery as I drive deeper into the forest. Oaks and evergreens line the long and windy dirt track leading the way to the prestigious Greenmount U.

I don't know what I expected, but it sure as hell wasn't a ghost town.

CHAPTER TEN
MILA

MILA: *Made it here safe and sound.*
Miss you already. I'll give you a call once I'm all settled in. x

I hit send on my message while praying Skye isn't going to be mad and hate me forever. Even though I'm only a couple of towns over, I know she's still pissed.

My best friend is proud of me, but she's still hurting and even though this is exciting for me, I need to remember her feelings are valid too. It doesn't matter what I say to her, Skye feels like I've ditched her.

The ultimate betrayal.

That's not the case and she knows it deep down. I'd never be able to do that to her because I know better than most that betrayal and neglect hits hard.

Maybe I'll Invite her over once I've had a chance to settle in and then she'll see that I haven't ditched her. Me and Skye, were in this life together. Through thick and thin, good and bad and nothing will be able to change that. The bond that binds us is unbreakable. Time or distance can never come between us. She's my soul sister and if anything, this is going to make us stronger in the long run.

I drive into campus, and it's like a completely different world. Ravendale, our local college, is your typical setup, but Greenmount is something else. This place is more like a manor, hidden away for only the elite to see.

The grounds are pristine. Everything is laid out in perfect sync. Where the leaves on the trees outside the grounds are green, inside Cherry blossoms are scattered around and I feel like I've been transported into a movie. A movie I never want to come out of.

As my trusty truck groans out as I drive deeper into the complex, I suddenly feel out of place. I need to get a new ride and fast before I become the new laughingstock of the place. I love my truck, and she's always been good to me. In a deadbeat town like Coldwater, I didn't think twice about driving around in a rust bucket—my sole purpose was to get to school, work and back in one piece, but I can already tell she isn't' going to cut it here.

I add new car to my never ending mental to do list and focus on the task at hand. A large marble water fountain comes into view, positioned slap bang in the middle of a perfectly landscaped lawn. This place is like a little slice of heaven and it's going to take an absolute lifetime for me to get used to it, but even then, I don't think that will be long enough.

I reach across the dash and pull out the map which was included in my welcome pack and I'd be lying if I said I wasn't overwhelmed. I can see the main building in front of me, but I'm at a loss with everything else. Where I assumed there would be dorm rooms like Ravendale, instead, a multitude of apartments are laid out all across campus.

I drove around a couple of times, trying to locate Apartment 8. It takes me longer than expected as they're not placed in numerical order, which to me would make more sense, but who am I to judge? I'm just the student.

After driving around in circles for twenty minutes, I finally found apartment 8. Whoever labelled this place as an apartment needs their eyes testing because this place is more than double the size of my mom's apartment. This is a frickin' house. A two-story house.

My guess is I won't be getting all this space to myself. I guess I'll be sharing with at least two to four other people and I inwardly groan. I shouldn't be ungrateful. It doesn't matter who I end up sharing with, at least I no longer have to go back to my mom's.

It doesn't take all too long to unpack my belongings given I didn't have a lot of treasured possessions or belongings to begin with. I grab the final box from my truck before slamming the door shut with my hip. Shrugging my duffel bag up my shoulder, I stand tall and take in my new life.

Four boxes await me at the door, plus the one in my hands. Some people might think I like to travel light, but the sad truth is, my whole life is in these boxes and my duffel... every last little thing I have to my name. I might not have much, but what I do have I've made sure I've provided it all for myself. I point blank refused to ask my mom for anything. No way would I willingly put myself in a position where she'd be able to use it against me.

I learned from a young age that the only person I can truly depend on in this life is me. If I want something and I want it bad enough, then it's down to me to make sure I get it. If not then I decide it's a luxury and not a necessity and it can wait until I can afford it.

My mouth opens in amazement, stunned that I'll be calling this place home for the next nine months. It really feels like I've left my reality and walked into a completely parallel universe.

From the outside, it looks so big and inviting.

Each apartment is two story's and situated on freshly cut green grass. A large drive is attached to each property, no doubt to accommodate the student vehicles. A black Jeep commander is parked on my drive and my heart drops to my stomach. Please don't tell me I'm sharing an apartment with someone who has a drink or drug problem. I don't think I'll be able to handle that kind of torture.

What if they have anger issues? Or worse... What If I'm forced to live with a bunch of plastic air heads. I have to deal with enough of them when I'm working at Frankie's. Yes, I know I shouldn't be ungrateful. Believe me, I'm beyond thankful for my blessings. I know how lucky I am to have secured a place here. But everyone has their preferences, right?

Sliding my key into the door, my heart swells, beating heavily and pumping pure adrenaline around my body as it fits into the slot and clicks when I turn it anti-clockwise. Just another small, yet majorly massive thing which proves this isn't another one of my wild and far-fetched daydreams.

I step inside, slowly placing one foot in front of the other, carefully placing my boxes inside and a huge smile takes over my face.

This is insane.

A huge open plan living area greets me, decorated with neutrals. It's fucking huge. A little intimidating but inviting at the same time. I'm sure with a little time I'll find a way to get used to it.

Now the fun really begins. Closing the door, I leave my bags in the hall, quickly deciding that the mundane task of unpacking can wait until later.

As I move silently into the apartment, it seems like no one else has arrived yet, and I have this place all to myself.

Never ever in my life have I ever had a space to myself so I'm going to make the most of it while I can. The hidden adventurer in me springs to life as I continue to walk across the wooden floor and come to a stop at what I'm guessing is the shared kitchen. I find a decent-sized utility room to my right and a compact bathroom to my left.

I'm eager to check out my room, taking the stairs two at a time.

The first door I stumble across is slightly ajar and when I take a quick look inside, I can see that this one is already taken. The room looks bare at first sight but I notice a few boxes here and there.

Not wanting to intrude, I take a step back and pull the door back, just how I found it before moving further down the narrow hall. It doesn't take me long before I come across another door. Again, this one also looks taken. Maybe I should have moved my stuff in yesterday and I would have had first dibs.

Anxiety ripples deep in my stomach when I quickly realize that I was right. This is a shared apartment, with a mix of boys and girls. It's no big deal, so long as whoever they are, they decide to stay out of my way.

I'm not here to make friends. I'm here to learn and make something of my life. I've always been good when it comes to keeping myself to myself, so it shouldn't be much of an issue on my part.

CHAPTER ELEVEN
JETT

It feels good to be back on campus. Back where I belong. Going back home, paying a visit to my mom was what I needed, but after spending time with Sienna, I was also reminded that I value my freedom. Not that I'll get much freedom now she's gonna be on my back twenty-four seven.

I still have no idea how she ended up securing a place at Greenmount. I hands down thought she would have enrolled at Ravendale, but then Sienna's always loved being full of surprises.

'Don't just stand there.' I bark out to the brunette standing by my bed. 'You weren't this shy ten minutes ago.'

If I remember correctly, she was the one who was waiting outside the apartment, desperate to make a move on me, to shoot her shot... and who am I to turn her down? After a shit-fest of a weekend, unable to remove Mila and her smart-ass mouth from my mind, I decided I'd deserved a break. A welcome and very much needed distraction.

I walk toward her, my huge frame towering over her small, shaking body. I reach out, my hand stroking her cheek, and her brown eyes grow wide. 'You scared, biscuit?' Defiance blazes in her eyes as she stands tall, trying to prove that she isn't scared of me. That she can handle all of me.

'You don't scare me' she says and there is zero conviction in her voice as a small quiver escapes her lips.

I raise my eyebrows, moving closer to her. 'You sure about that?' I question. pushing my hands into my shorts. I grab my dick and set it free, watching this puck bunny stare at me open mouthed. I slide my hands up and down my shaft, feeling it grow beneath my touch, and a blaze of heat rushes to her cheeks. 'It's not too late to back out.' I warn.

She shakes her head, before biting down nervously on her bottom lip. She doesn't answer me, instead to my surprise she drops down to her knees, kneeling before me, ready to worship me like the God I truly am.

'Fuck my mouth, Jett.' She looks up at me through her lashes. 'I want to taste you on my tongue.' Her tone is pleading. She's desperate for me and this excites me more.

I'm not the type of guy who needs telling twice. She opens her mouth, welcoming me freely, the heat of her tongue consumes me, and I throw my head back, thrusting deeper, losing myself in another desperate chick who can't seem to stay away from me.

All too soon she pulls away and a small gasp sounds out around us, her eyes wide with fear, almost like she's seen a ghost. Quickly realizing something is off, I turn my head, facing her line of sight and I freeze momentarily, my mouth falling open as I take in the delicious sight before me.

'Like what you see, princess?' I growl out, raising one eyebrow, silently daring her smart-ass mouth to argue with me, but it falls flat. Mila doesn't answer me, instead her stormy hazel eyes flit between the brunette on her knees and my solid cock, and my skin tingles with heat, adrenaline and anticipation.

My mind veers off, the brunette instantly forgotten as I focus all my attention on Mila, suddenly imagining what her smart-ass mouth would feel like wrapped around my dick, and my chest-rises and falls rapidly, my heart rate running dangerously high.

'What are you doing here?' She stammers, a rush of heat flustering her cheeks. She's embarrassed. She's vulnerable as she looks at me and it drives me insane. A victorious smile dances onto my face. Pure satisfaction that I'm still able to get a reaction out of her. Even when my dick is in some random chick's mouth.

I watch as she swallows down hard. 'Don't just stand there, princess. Come and join in.' my grip tightens around my dick, stroking up and down, refusing to break eye contact with her. 'There's plenty to go around.'

CHAPTER TWELVE
MILA

MILA: I take it back. I'm so ready to come back to Coldwater.

Seriously, I haven't even started yet, and you are not going to believe what's just happened to me... Call me ASAP. X

I hit send, my hands shaking, and my heart is racing deep inside my chest. My eyes refusing to unsee the image which has just been burned to the back of my eyelids for all eternity.

I swear, I wouldn't be able to make it up even if I tried. Images of Jett's naked body run around vividly on repeat, crystal clear without any censors. My skin tingles, a rush of desire pooling at my core as I'm reminded of how his jade green eyes burned into me, intensely. Melting me from just his look alone as he looked deep down into the very depths of my shattered soul.

A part of me shouldn't have been shocked at his predatorial delight when I walked into what should be my room. Any normal person would have been embarrassed to be caught in that kind of situation, maybe even apologized—but not Jett.

If anything, I'd bet finding me standing there as he violated some girl's mouth with his solid dick, my mouth wide open, rooted to the spot with no place to go, my body succumbing to shock no doubt gave him an added thrill. An extra kick to his sick and twisted mind. My untimely appearance probably spurred him on some more.

I knew he wasn't someone to be messed with when I saw him down at the Lake party last night. Hell, he as good as told me so with his predatorial stance and the dangerous warning in his eyes. But in my defense, I was sincerely hoping our paths wouldn't ever cross again.

Yeah... I should be so lucky. What the hell am I supposed to do now? Less than thirty minutes in and Jett has already ruined the new chapter in my life.

It's my first day at Greenmount. I should be happy, beyond ecstatic. I should be busy unpacking my few belongings right now, focusing on settling into my new apartment, but it sure looks like my new roommate had other ideas. Not good ideas by the looks of things seeing how she's already decided to hook up with Greenmount's very own fuck boy.

A cold shiver of unease ripples down my spine when I realize I'm expected to go back in there as soon as they've had their nasty time.

No way am I sleeping in that room. No fucking way. I don't care if they bleach the place from top to bottom, until their hands are red-raw, I'm still not sleeping in that room. The girl with the loose panties has already made herself at home in there, so she can take her belongings and move into that room permanently.

I'd be more than happy to take one of the other rooms, but how do I know she hasn't been up to no good in those too?

If it comes to it, I'd have no problem living in my truck.

What an epic start to my new life. It doesn't matter where I go, there's always someone on the sidelines just waiting to fuck me over.

Thankfully I don't get too much time to dwell on the issue when my phone suddenly vibrates in my back pocket. I expect to see Skye's name flashing back at me after my SOS message, but a heavy sigh escapes me when I see a different name altogether, and I lean back against my truck, feeling all defeated all over again.

Should I even bother answering? My day has already gone to shit so what's another problem added to my never-ending list?

I hit the green button before chickening out and pull my phone up to my ear before I close my eyes. 'Hello,' I say down the line, my voice completely void of any emotion, instantly regretting my decision to answer it.

'Hey babe...' Nausea twists my stomach at the sound of his voice, quickly replacing the butterflies which used to reside there. 'Where you at?'

Is this some kind of joke? 'What do you mean where am I at?'

'Exactly what I said. I'm outside your place, and your truck's not here.' No fucking shit. 'Are you at Frankie's?' He presses. 'I didn't check because I didn't think you did day shifts.'

'I don't.' I reply in a clipped voice. Pinching the bridge of my nose, I throw my head back, praying to all things holy that I somehow manage to keep hold of my limited composure. 'I'm not at Frankie's until tonight.'

A rush of disbelief and anger courses through my overly strong body, refusing to believe he could be so forgetful. Cole has always been all for himself. But even this is another level for him.

'What do you want?' I press, coaxing him to get to the point of his pointless phone call.

Silence trickles down the line before he finally clears his throat. 'Alright, I'm gonna be up front with you, babe.' He is? Damn, this must be a first. 'I hate it when we argue.' Him and me both, but this time it's all on Cole. He's the one to blame for the fallout, not me. 'I thought maybe we could meet up, grab some lunch and talk things through before I head back to Ravendale tomorrow.'

'Sounds great.' I say, the heavy sarcasm falling off my tongue, but Cole's too self-absorbed to pick up on it. 'Do you even know where I am?' I demand, kicking the gravel beneath my feet, wishing it was Cole's stupid face.

'No,' he laughs. 'that's the reason I'm calling you, obvs.'

Nothing and I mean nothing will ever change his obnoxious, self-entitled ways. I don't even know what I saw in him except a distraction from my horrible and traumatic life back at home, but it turns out Cole is no better for me anyways.

'I'm busy.' is all I manage to say before swallowing down hard on the lump of emotion which has appeared at the back of my throat. I've wasted so much time on Cole over the years, giving him pointless chance after pointless chance, hoping and praying one day he might actually grow the hell up and change, but deep down I've come to the harsh realization that Cole will never change. He'll always be out for himself and I'm so over it.

I never openly admitted it to myself but I put up with endless bullshit because I didn't want to be alone. I'd rather be with someone who devalued my worth just so I felt loveable.

Just another post traumatic response following years of neglect from my mom.

'Busy?' He snaps back, clearly pissed he's no longer in the loop. All traces of his fake nice persona have vanished, his true colors finally back on show. 'Busy doing what, and with who?' I don't miss the accusation in his tone, and even though his lack of trust stings me a little, I decide right in this moment that I'm so done with him and his self-centered bullshit.

'You've already forgotten, haven't you?' I confirm, wondering how he could possibly forget the one thing, the main reason he decided to walk out on me in the first place.

'Forgotten what?' He asks. I shake my head and look up to the cloudy sky, searching in vain for answers. Answers which will never materialize. 'I've left, Cole.' My voice is surprisingly calm when I deliver the news. 'I'm at Greenmount.' As expected, a heavy silence fills the line for a few moments and I can visualize his angular face, scrunched in annoyance. Totally pissed that I continued on my journey, going completely against his wishes.

Cole needs to remember that he doesn't own me. This is my life. My dream, and I'm here to chase it, no matter where it might lead me. I don't want to wake up one day in forty to fifty years' time, lay in bed, riddled with regret from the chances and risks I didn't take because some guy of the moment didn't like or agree with my decision.

Hell no.

The way I see it is this; if Cole cared about me at all, he'd man up and get over his jealousy and silly boy issues. He'd have my back and he'd be more than happy to cheer me on from the sidelines all day long.

It's perfectly clear for me to see now that Cole has never had my back, nor my best interests at heart. Now I've taken a much-needed step back I can see his true colors; colors I'm not all too fond of.

'Are you shittin' me?' His voice is icy cold as it blows down the line, and I barely recognize it. I knew he'd be pissed but I sure as hell didn't expect him to turn so cold on me. 'So that's it then...'

'Don't get-funny, Cole. I already told you I wasn't going to change my mind.' My own voice falters and I hate that he can still turn his bullshit attitude around on me. I haven't done anything wrong, but Cole loves to play the role of an innocent victim.

This is my future we're talking about here. Not his. Cole is already set-up. He's good to go with a scholarship at Ravendale. Cole's life has been far from hard or challenging. He was born with a massive silver spoon in his mouth and everything else he's ever needed has been handed to him on a golden plate ever since. But I've never once judged him for it.

I've always been little miss independent and I never saw that as a bad thing.

Maybe that could be one of my downfalls, but I guess that's what happens when you've been left to fend for yourself. I had my whole childhood ripped away from me at a young age all because of my mom. But again, I'm not bitter. I make sure I get up each and every day and try to do better than the last, and I'm so proud of myself for how far I've come.

I could have crumbled. I could have easily given up and kept my head in the past, but I'm a fighter. A true survivor.

'I don't understand. You had everything you needed at Ravendale.' He hisses. 'There was no reason for you to pack up and go to Greenmount.' And this moment is when I finally realize he doesn't know me at all.

Cole knows the issues I'm faced with on a daily basis when it comes to my mom and her never-ending demons and battles.

'You know why I had to leave.' I remind him and my voice breaks, laced with heavy emotion that I shouldn't be feeling as I'm forced once again to explain myself to someone who refuses to listen. To Cole Williams: the master of manipulation.

'Thats real nice, Mila. Look, I know you have it real hard sometimes...' *Sometimes?* Is he fucking kidding me? Every single day of my depressing existence has been a headache. Cole doesn't even know half of it. Maybe if he'd actually been around more, maybe then he'd be able to take a step back and appreciate just how bad a hand I've actually been dealt. 'I'm sorry I wasn't enough for you to stay.'

Before I have a chance to say anything else, the line drops and there's nothing but a deathly silence on the other end.

I don't even have the energy to be mad.

My whole body is numb. What a brilliant start to my new beginning. Deep down I know seeing the back of Cole will be good for me in the long run. It just might take me a little time to process and adjust to life without him in it. Even though he's a grade A Jerk, Cole has been my crutch for so long, and even though deep down I know he's no good for me, I'm going to have to learn to walk all over again... to find my balance: All by myself.

CHAPTER THIRTEEN
MILA

I don't know how long I've been hiding out in my truck. Minutes, maybe hours... who knows, but one thing I do know is that I can't stay out here forever.

I'm going to have to step inside the apartment at some point. I'm going to have to face the music eventually and I already know it isn't going to be fun, or pretty.

I reached out to Skye, the number one solver of most of my problems, leaving multiple missed calls and messages, but I'm yet to hear back from her.

I'm happy to pretend she's busy instead of admitting she's ignoring me. Either way, I'm left with no choice but to sort this bullshit mess out on my own.

I jump out of my skin, my heart skyrocketing in my chest when a loud knock sounds out on my window. If Jett seriously thinks he can walk over to me, try to explain himself now he's had his fun and been sucked dry, then he can give his ego-tastic head a wobble and think again.

I don't want to listen to anything he has to say. I won't even be able to bring myself to look at him again, especially now I've seen him in all his beautiful naked glory. My heart skips a beat just thinking about it.

'Mila, right?' The voice calls out, slowly flowing through my open window. When I look up, I've never been so relieved in my life when I see someone other than Jett and his current fuck piece.

'Right.' I reply before offering Sienna a weak smile. Her brows furrow as she takes me in, trying to understand why I'm still in my truck when I should be getting familiar with my new apartment and what campus has to offer.

As if magically reading her mind she says, 'What are you doing out here?' Her blue eyes filled with a deep curiosity. What do I do in this situation? Do I make up a quick lie and hope she's gullible enough to buy it, hopefully biding me some much-needed time in the process, or should I take the bull by the horns and tell her the truth, that my new roommate has fully acquainted herself with her arch nemesis? I quickly decide on the former—the latter being way too embarrassing, especially given that as nice as she may seem; I still don't know her all too well.

'Just waiting on a phone call...' I hope my voice sounds convincing enough.

'Mom checking up on you?' Her question is innocent enough but I'd be lying if I said it didn't hurt a little. 'My mom was on my case before I was off the driveway.'

'Something like that.' I mutter, knowing all too well that my mom is probably still face down, sleeping off last night's session.

'So, are you all settled in?' I ask, desperate to change the current topic of conversation.

Her whole face lights up, beaming with excitement as she takes me in, and her smile is contagious. 'Hell no, but I will be soon enough.' She nods to her car, parked a small distance behind mine. 'But I need food and lots of it before I even think about unloading my stuff.' She pauses a moment, then says, 'Why don't you come with me, roomie.'

'Roomie?' Now it's my turn to raise my brow in shock.

'Apartment 8?' All I can do is nod. 'Me too.'

A small sense of relief courses through me that I'll actually know someone not just on campus, but who I'll be living with. Now it won't just be me and the sex crazed nympho.

'Food?' Sienna asks again.

'I'm good.' The actual truth is any hunger I felt instantly vanished when I saw Jett with his dick in some girl's mouth. But I don't feel comfortable telling Sienna that little tidbit of information.

'You sure? I bet you're starving.'

'Seriously, I'm okay.'

'Sure you are. If it's about the phone call you're waiting on, there's a little secret I'm gonna let you in on...'

'Which is...' I say feigning curiosity.

'They're mobile which means you can take them anywhere and still receive calls. Any place, any time. Cool, huh?'

Well, that's me screwed. Sienna has me cornered, caught-in her trap. One I can't really get out of. But on the other hand, walking off with Sienna could be just what I need. It will give me a reason to step away from the apartment, sparing myself heaps of embarrassment in the long run.

Here's hoping Jett will be long gone by the time I get back, and then I'll try to set some house rules, some much needed boundaries with the sex pest vacating my room.

CHAPTER FOURTEEN
MILA

I spent the majority of the afternoon walking around campus with Sienna. She showed me the places where the cool kids hung out and she also showed me the places I needed to avoid. Considering she's a first year too she sure knew a lot about Greenmount. I tried to coax her out of information but she remained tight-lipped, reminding me that a lady never tells her secrets.

Time went by pretty fast and I'll always be forever grateful that she helped out a girl in need and kept my mind thoroughly occupied. I didn't even have time to head back to the apartment to unpack my belongings but I'll take that as a blessing in disguise. I don't have the energy to deal with little miss no panties. If I'm lucky, by the time my shift has ended, maybe she'll be tucked up in bed and I won't have to face her until tomorrow at least.

Thankfully, I was granted another small mercy by the God's and I managed to avoid the hot as hell weird guy who likes to get his dick out to anyone. If Skye were here, she would have taken a ride on him already. I clench my teeth at the thought as an intense bitterness invades my mouth. I'd like to put it down to anger at the thought of Jett devaluing my best friend like that, but I'm kidding myself. Jealousy has never held a part of my world, but the thought of Jett going near my best friend has me green with envy.

I don't even know the guy, yet he's somehow managed to evoke all kinds of emotions within me and I really don't like it, or the power this dark and brooding stranger has over me. I'm acting reckless, allowing my wild and unruly thoughts to wander to places they don't belong.

Not for the first time today have I found myself wishing that I was the girl on the floor, succumbing to Jett's demands as he invaded my mouth with his solid erection.

I have no idea who he is. All I know is that he's bad news and I need to stay out of his way at all costs. Not because I don't trust him. No, the hard truth is that I don't trust myself when I'm around him.

He's dangerous, and he's no good for an innocent girl like me.

I hit a right into Coldwater and my mood instantly shifts. Like I've just driven through the fog of doom, the sudden shift in the atmosphere is instant, and it doesn't feel like I've been away at all. As crazy as it seems, especially after today's eye-opening events, a small part of me has missed this miserable, mundane town.

On my drive over I decided to go by my mom's, unable to stop myself from checking up on her, if only from a distance. I know I said I was going to keep away, but old habits sure die hard.

The house looked empty. No lights were on, signaling that she's gone elsewhere to find her next fix. No doubt Dan has dragged her sorry ass off to one of his other deadbeat associates. I should feel bad, but my mom is old enough and stupid enough to make her own mistakes.

She can't keep leaning on me forever.

'Here she is...' Skye shouts the moment I walk through the diner doors, and she's positioned at the bar as usual. I walk over to her and all she can do is smile, but I don't return her energy. 'Where were you?' I demand.

'Oh yeah, about that...' she begins but I'm not in the mood to hear her out. I've had the day from hell, and she was nowhere to be found.

'I really needed you today.' I confess and for some strange reason I feel exposed, vulnerable, totally not myself.

Skye watches me, amusement dancing in her big brown eyes. 'Greenmount not what you expected?' The glee in her voice is evident and this does nothing to improve my mood.

'Something like that. Hang on, why are you looking so pleased with yourself?' There's a certain sparkle in Skye's eyes and her cheeks are flushed. 'What have you been doing?' I question, knowing all too well what that look represents. Skye has been busy... too busy to come to her best friend's rescue. She's been too busy with a boy.

'Your girl might have had a date.' Another blush rushes to her cheeks. *Un-fucking- believable.*

'I thought you'd put an end to things with Shawn?' I raise my eyes suspiciously, unable to keep up with Skye and her over-the-top antics.

'Shawn?' she exclaims as though saying his name has just insulted her mouth. Shawn's long gone. That prick had his chance and he blew it good and proper.'

'Then who?' she waggles her eyebrows at me, once again looking super pleased with herself.

'Now that would be telling. I don't want to jinx it too soon, you know.' my eyes grow wider, like she's just slapped me across the face.

'Skye, you can't keep those kinds of details from me. I'm your best friend. There's no secrets between the two of us...'

'I can,' she points her finger at me and I don't like this whole new attitude she has going on. 'And I will...'

'But...'

'But nothing. I have to get used to days without you by my side,' Oh, here comes the guilt card. The ace she'll keep up her sleeve, keeping it on standby, ready to pull it out and disarm me at a moment's notice.

'Are you really going to begrudge me a little fun, a welcome distraction while you're off doing your own thing?'

I don't even bother giving her an answer. I know what she's doing. She's still mad at me. This is Skye's way of acting out. Trying to put on a front while making me feel bad in the process.

'I need to get ready for work.' I sigh, realizing I'm not about to get anywhere fast with her tonight. Skye is the most stubborn person I know, and she can hold a grudge like no other. I'll bide my time. I'm more than happy to wait it out until she's eventually gotten over her little bitch fit... however long that might be.

Skye doesn't give me any more snide remarks which I'm thankful for. She's far too busy in her own mind, living out her date with Mr. Mystery. I have no idea who he is, or where she found him, and there's no way she's going to willingly let me in on the details while she's still pissed with me.

My heart stops when the diner door opens and I find Cole standing there, arm in arm with some random girl from Ravendale. What the hell does he think he's playing at? Everything stops, my erratic heart thudding in my ears as I refuse to take in the sight before me.

After what feels like a lifetime, Cole looks around the diner and when his eyes find mine his mouth opens, but the sleazy jerk quickly closes it again.

I don't even know what I'm supposed to do in this situation. Do I scream? Do I shout? All I want to do is reach behind the bar and throw something heavy at his arrogant face. Something which will wipe the smile off his face for good.

I don't know what comes over me. Maybe it's a buildup of all the bullshit I've been forced to deal with, and I'm so fed up with being used as a dirty welcome mat, where people continue to walk over me, regardless of how I feel.

I wait until his side piece walks toward a booth and I make my way over to him, my footsteps silent and deadly as I move across the diner. I know Cole, and the last thing he'd expect is for me to confront him—especially in public. Obviously, Cole doesn't know the first thing about me and that says a hell of a lot more about him and his actions than it does me.

'So, this is how it's going to be?' My voice holds a lot more strength and conviction than I initially anticipated, and I'm proud of myself for holding my own and standing my ground.

'What do you mean?' Cole hurls back, his cocky arrogance oozing out of every pore and he makes me sick to my stomach. 'You're the one who decided to leave.' He snarls, like this is justification for him moving on so fast. That's if he hadn't already been doing the dirty behind my back.

'I've gone to Greenmount, Cole. That didn't mean I was jumping on a plane and leaving the country.' Although that thought sounds appealing right now. 'I wasn't leaving you.'

'As good as,' he snaps back. 'I didn't expect to see you here...'

'I told you I was working before.' I remind him. 'But that just shows you never listen to anything I say. It didn't take you long to move on either.'

His black eyes hold me captive as they burn into me. 'Maybe you should try it,' his voice is cold and completely void of any emotion. All I can do is stand in the middle of Frankie's, my mouth open in shock, rendered speechless by this heartless son of a bitch who is supposed to be my boyfriend.

Without another word I'm forced to watch as he turns away, walks over to the booth and leans in to kiss his new plaything.

Deep down, somewhere hidden beneath the pain and humiliation, I know I'm worth so much more. I know I'll be better off without him in the long run. I just have to keep reminding myself.

CHAPTER FIFTEEN
MILA

My blood is still boiling, bubbling deep under the surface, threatening to erupt and consume every fiber of my being. who the fuck does Cole think he is. I know he wanted a reaction from me. I know he wanted to hurt me the way I've hurt him. I get it, but it still doesn't make it right. I might have unintentionally hurt Cole, but I'd never dreamed of humiliating him. Especially the way he humiliated me tonight.

Cole knew I'd be a Frankie's.

I as good as told him so before, and when he'd found out I'd stuck to my plans, dead set on heading to Greenmount; when he realized I wasn't about to put my life on hold, that's when he must have devised his plan. Cole had every intention of humiliating me tonight, and I have to admit, he did an epic job.

For the first time since I started working at Frankie's, I couldn't wait for my shift to end. I couldn't wait to get out of there. If the humiliation wasn't enough to contend with, all I could feel were endless heated stares from the kids hanging out in the booths.

Cole's minions.

Now I'm driving back to Greenmount and I'm dreading what's waiting for me back at the apartment. I'm hopeful that Jett would have had his fill of my roommate and I won't be forced to face him anytime soon. It's late, so I'm also praying that said roommate will be tucked up fast asleep in bed.

I don't think I'll survive any more drama tonight.

***

The lights are out when I make it back to the apartment and relief floods out of my body. Thankfully, I'm not going to have to face little miss desperate. I'm sure once I've had a good night's sleep, I might feel brave enough to face her over breakfast tomorrow. But then on second thought, I don't think I'll be able to face her without picturing Jett's cock in her mouth.

I take a moment to collect my thoughts and try to process the events of the past twenty-four hours. I swear, I couldn't even make this shit up. Here I was thinking I was about to start some epic new adventure, only to end up witnessing some random guy's dick being shoved down some girl's throat, followed by an argument with my ex that I didn't need... then the icing on the cake was watching my ex parade his new fuck piece around my place of work. I never thought I could be humiliated so many times in one day.

I finally find the strength to climb out of my truck just as another loud clap of thunder booms out above my head, and the heavens open up around me.

I run to the door, scrambling in my bag trying to find my keys before I end up drenched. Thankfully luck seems to be on my side, and I'm inside the apartment in seconds. I switch on the lights but nothing happens. Great, the power is out. Fucking perfect. Like I haven't dealt with enough bullshit today, now I need to try and navigate my way around an apartment I'm unfamiliar with in the dark.

Placing my hands on the ball, I feel around me as I try to remember that lay out I saw this morning. The ferocious wind rattles the windowpane and all the hairs on the back of my neck stand tall, and I instantly know I'm not alone.

I have a flashlight on my phone. I pull it from my pocket and my heart sinks some more when I realize the battery is flat. I've been out all day and didn't get the chance to charge it. I'm screwed. All I know is that I'm somewhere in the hallway. I don't know where the stairs are from memory and my anxiety skyrockets.

I hear someone move behind me and I instantly freeze on the spot, desperately hoping that this isn't a human hiding out in the dark and one of my new roommates has brought a pet along for the ride.

I try to turn but feel something hard and warm press up against me as an intoxicating scent of Cedarwood consumes me. I'm not alone, and I know who's behind me. I can't see him, but I can feel the heat of his minty breath tickling my neck as he whispers, 'Scared of the storm, princess?'

His voice has me in a chokehold. It's predatorial, husky and laced with a savage hunger, and my breathing quickens in response. I swallow down hard, unable to answer him, knowing all too well that I'm trapped.

A soft chuckle escapes him and he moves closer to me, his string athletic body flush against mine and I feel his solid erection pressing into my back. 'It's not the storm you should be scared of princess. Not when I have you all alone in this apartment.'

'What are you doing here?' I demand on a breathless whisper. 'You should have left ages ago.' I try to sound strong and unaffected by his domineering presence, but we both know I'm failing miserably.

'Why wouldn't I be here? This is my apartment too.' He growls out before pressing his warm and welcoming lips onto the soft skin at my neck. I can't move. I'm frozen, rooted to the spot as a mixture of fear and excitement courses through my body and I unwillingly go lax under his touch.

Everything about this whole situation is wrong. So fucking wrong, but after the shit-fest of a day I've had, it also feels so fucking right.

I'm usually the shy one, but maybe it's time I took a leaf out of Cole's book and began to live a little. Maybe I should do as he asked and move on. I throw my head back as Jett's vicious mouth wreaks havoc on my body, and this time I don't try to stop him. Instead, I close my eyes and lose myself in all things Jett Jameson.

After all, what's one night of fun? It doesn't have to mean anything.

My body instantly responds to his touch and before I know what's happening, Jett has me pinned up against the wall, cocooned in his big arms. A rush of desire ripples through my body as his expert touch sends shockwaves through me and a pool of desire rushes to my core.

I don't think I have ever wanted anyone as much as I want Jett in this moment.

This is a once in a lifetime event, never to be repeated so I'm going to make sure I enjoy every last second of it, then neither of us will ever speak of it again.

CHAPTER SIXTEEN
JETT

When my eyes open and I slowly return to the land of the living, I instantly know something is different. Something is off. The atmosphere in my room is electric, not its usual sense of calm.

My mind is still hazy from sleep, and it takes me a good minute to gather and collect my racing thoughts... and when my mind slowly settles and begins to calm, a wild rush of images from the events of last night push to the surface, swimming to the forefront of my mind.

The storm...

The blackout...

Waiting not so patiently for Mila to come back to the apartment...

Ever since she walked in on me with my dick down some random chick's throat, I haven't been able to erase her horrified and furious expression from my mind. And fuck, did I try. She was just another chick; one with a smart-ass mouth, and she didn't deserve any space inside my head. No one does, so why should she be any different?

Mila was all I could think about and the longer she kept me waiting the more impatient and worked up I became.

My mood worsened some more when I fast realized that Sienna would not only be joining me at Greenmount, but in a sick twist of fate, she's also one of my new roomies too. Just when I think the universe can't fuck me over any more than it already has, she decides to throw another bitch fit and punch me in the balls at the same time.

No matter what I try to do, I Just can't seem to catch a break at the minute.

Sienna's sudden appearance didn't last all too long. As soon as the storm hit, Sienna, materialistic to the core, quickly decided to drive back to mom's. A life without light, internet and trash Tv is a life Sienna doesn't want to be a part of, and that was more than okay with me.

A life without Sienna on my case sounds perfect to me, but I couldn't enjoy the peace and quiet because Mila was running around in my head on repeat. I Just couldn't shut her down, no matter how hard I tried.

Mason: my right-hand man isn't coming to Greenmount until tomorrow. Some family emergency had prevented him from arriving yesterday. I should have called him, checked he was okay, but then the storm hit, cutting everything off. That's when I decided to convince myself I wasn't a bad friend, we both just needed a little headspace. I convinced myself I'd be fine, back to the good old Jett Jameson everyone knew and loved again as soon as I'd managed to speak to Mila.

I needed to see her.

I needed to talk to her—face to face.

If she was going to be living here then I needed to make sure the ground rules were placed, set and firmly cemented. Little miss smart mouth needs to know where she stands. She needs to learn what's expected of her, especially if she's going to be living under the same roof as me.

I'd love to say that's exactly what happened when she finally rocked up at stupid O'clock this morning, but then I'd be lying.

I allow my mind one last run of the memory before shutting it back down, storing it away safely, so I can come back to it at a later date.

Rolling over onto my back, I throw my hands behind my head. What hole have I gone and dug for myself now? I have no idea who Mila is, but she's for real having a crazy ass effect on me. Usually I'm a fuck 'em and chuck 'em kind of guy, but shit, I'd happily go for another ride with her sweet tight little pussy again... *and again... and again.*

It's unheard of for me. I've always lived by one rule: one pussy—one night. There's enough to go around, but now I've had a taste of Mila, nothing else will do. No other girl on this campus or surrounding areas will hold the same appeal, and even though it sounds fucked up, I'm surprised to find I'm totally here for it.

I breathe in deep as my mind wanders to Sienna and her diva ways. My little sister is going to lose her shit when she comes back from mom's and learns what I've done. Sure, its' no secret that I'll fuck anyone with a pussy—all except one, and I've never once given a moment's thought to the consequences of my actions... until now.

Sienna's going to hunt me down and she won't stop until she has my balls as a victorious prize for my downfall. Sienna made her intentions clear at the Lake party. Mila is her friend and now they're roomies. The perfect situation for Sienna to find herself in... me, not so much.

No, the big bad wolf has gone and done the unthinkable. I've gone and fucked her new friend.

I fucked Mila and I fucked her good. It's not like she's going to forget me any time soon, and I don't want her to. But Sienna, there's no way she'll see this the same way as me. No fucking way.

Maybe Mila might do the unthinkable and keep her mouth closed. Maybe she'll surprise me and turn out different from the rest of these desperate puck bunnies... the very ones who love nothing more than to gossip and compare their meaningless one night of fun with me.

I can wish all I damn well like, but the bottom line is, Mila is a chick, just the same as all the rest and there's no way, no way in hell that she'll be able to keep quiet.

A flicker of movement catches my attention, a shadow creeping into my peripheral and it takes me a minute to realize what's happening.

Shit.

What the hell have I gone and done?

I'm Jett Jameson, a man of many talents and endless chick's to choose from. I don't have the time or patience to invest in anyone other than thyself, and above all else I set myself rules for a reason. Solid boundaries that I'll always adhere to. I'm disciplined. I'm always in control. Jett Jameson doesn't dip the same pussy twice and I don't do sleepovers, period.

So why the fuck is there some random chick splayed out, butt naked in my bed?

My heart stops, sinking deeper into my stomach when I take a closer look, my eyes fixed on her creamy flesh and honey blonde hair, I quickly realize the girl in my bed isn't random at all.

The girl curled into my black satin sheets is none other than Mila.

Fuck...

She never left. She didn't get up and leave like they usually do. Like they're supposed to do. We both must have crashed at the same time. That's the only explanation my dumbfounded brain can come up with right now.

Panic quickly rushes in, my heartrate racing deep inside my aching chest as I wonder how this sudden and unexpected turn of events is about to play out.

Sure, I'm down for a good time, but never a long time. Fun is my middle name, but no one and I mean no one has ever stayed the night in my room, let alone in my fucking bed.

If this gets out, spread amongst the masses then I'm fucked. It will be game over for me. My reputation as Greenmount's number one fuckboy will be ruined. The guys will take the piss out of me and the girls, they'll think I'm pussy whipped; and that couldn't be any farther from the truth.

I'll never be pussy whipped, period.

I don't know what's happening. My head is all over the place. One thing I do know is I need to get out of here and fast.

I need to distance myself from this messed-up situation and clear my head. If I put some much-needed space between us maybe then I'll stand a better chance of trying to think straight-without any unwanted distractions.

I reluctantly turn my head to the side so I can face her. Face what I've done while still living in denial; refusing to believe that I was stupid enough, too pussy drunk to allow this to happen.

Even though Mila is right next to me. Even though I can see her, I'm still trying to convince myself that this isn't real and any minute now I'll wake up from this horrific nightmare and all will be right in my world again.

At least that's what I thought would happen, but when I look at her, when I watch her sleeping, her delicate heart shaped face all rested and peaceful, my heart does another unexpected flip and a wild rush of foreign emotions course through my body, freezing me in place, all intentions of escaping slowly declining by the second.

As much as I hate to admit it, Mila looks good in my bed. She looks pretty fucking good laying next to me, her beautiful body within touching distance, but against the odds I surprise myself by keeping my hands to myself.

Who even am I?

It's like I woke up a completely different guy and I'm still unsure how I feel about it. I'll be honest. Surprisingly, Mila looks in place, like she's where she needs to be and that bizarre thought sends my head into a total spin, going around and around without any sign of an emergency stop button.

This is all kinds of crazy.

Totally insane.

I have no idea what kind of charge was in the air last night, but it must have been potent because this isn't usually how I spend my mornings.

Deciding there's not much else I can do, I gently push myself up, trying to get out of bed without disturbing her. If I can make it to the bathroom before she wakes up then she'll never know I was here, in bed next to her. I'd pretend I'd played the inevitable gentleman and slept on the floor.

Maybe I could head downstairs before she catches a glimpse of me. For all Mila knows, I could have been the perfect gentleman and left as soon as I'd fucked her, all because she'd fallen asleep first and I didn't have the heart to disturb her.

Yeah, right... like anyone's going to buy that bullshit excuse. Especially from the likes of me.

Silence fills the air around us, broken only by Mila's faint breathing, indicating that I haven't disturbed her and she's still out cold, and a familiar rush of relief sweeps through me knowing that I might make it out of this mess unscathed. So long as no one catches me doing the walk of shame... out of my own fucking room.

'Oh my God.' She squeals, her high-pitched voice echoing around the room. Snapping my eyes to hers, she flinches back into the bed, realization seeping into her every pore as she pulls my sheets up and around her naked body, trying to shield herself from my hungry and predatorial gaze.

She wasn't all too worried about that last night and as if reading my mind, her cheeks flush crimson, the rush of her embarrassment dancing on her confused face. Damn, she looks so fuckable like this and I have to refrain myself, forcing myself to remain still so I don't lean across the bed and claim her as my own once more.

'Looking good, princess.' I say on a sinister snicker and a wicked grin curves the edges of my mouth. Mila is uncomfortable, that much is a given. Call me a sick and twisted son of a bitch all you like, but her fear and unease excites me like nothing before.

'I'm sorry...' she mumbles deep into the sheets, her voice so soft and small that I barely hear her. Her comment has thrown me and I furrow my brows in confusion. I don't think anyone has ever apologized to me in my room before. Mila is sure pulling a lot of firsts out of me, and I'm not sure I like it all too much.

'What are you apologizing for?' I question before I can stop myself.

'This... us... shit...' she stammers, struggling to string a simple sentence together. Mila clears her throat and tries again. 'Last night shouldn't have happened.'

I thought she'd say that. 'But it did.' I cut in, again unable to stop myself.

'No Shit. But it shouldn't have happened and now look at me...'

'Oh, believe me, I'm looking princess, and from where I'm positioned, you'll get no complaints from me.' I lick my bottom lip hungrily as I soak up the delicious sight of her and I'm shocked when I realize I could sit here all day long just looking at her in my bed, knowing the delights that await me, hidden beneath my sheets.

If she thinks they'll protect her from me then she's sadly mistaken.

'I'm in your bed... with nothing on.'

'Don't fucking remind me.' I warn her on a heated growl while my dick twitches to life. Can't she see how hard I'm struggling, desperately trying to keep a handle on my composure so I don't break another one of my golden rules.

'Is this some kind of fucked up joke to you?' She demands, her face stern and her jaw set, only the quiver in her voice showing a true sign of her emotions.

This is all kinds of new to me and I'm at a loss. I'm the master of control, a God amongst men. I can disarm any girl and charm her out of her panties with one look, but I can't handle the sight of Mila waking up in my bed.

'I'm not laughing.' I confirm, not sure why, I'm trying to defend myself but the words roll freely from my tongue, like she's laced me with truth serum. 'At least I'm not laughing at you.' When she narrows her eyes, I'm quick to add, 'look, buckle up buttercup because you won't hear me say this often, if ever, but right now I'm not mad about it. I'm not complaining. This sure beats the usual sight which greets me in the morning.'

She instantly flinches at my words, turning in on herself again and I realize how bad that probably sounded. 'I need to go.' she breathes on a whisper while refusing to meet my gaze.

'Hey, don't stress.' I hold my hands up, showing I don't mean her any harm. 'Don't worry about it. It's no big deal.' I try my best to reassure her but I get the heavy sense that I'm only digging myself into a deeper hole. A hole I have no idea how to get out of. The wording sounds all kinds of wrong, but in my defense, I've never had to speak to or explain myself to anyone else but my own reflection as soon as I wake up.

'No big deal... right.' She mutters some more as she slowly pulls herself into a sitting position and the sight of her pale creamy flesh, so close within touching distance does all things kind of crazy to me. 'Maybe not to you, but you need to realize I'm nothing like the usual girls who you seek out and prey on. I'm not like those girls who freely jump in your bed...'

Hell... She isn't fucking wrong there.

Last night shouldn't have meant anything to me. Last night shouldn't have been a big deal... but it was. More than I ever thought possible, but how the hell do I try to explain that without sounding like a total dick?

The damage has already been done and there's nothing I can do to change that. I can't turn back time and erase the events of last night or what unfolded afterward. And if truth be told, I don't think I'd want to change anything.

Before I have a chance to say anything else, Mila jumps off the bed, my black satin sheets wrapped tightly around her small hourglass frame before making a run for it—straight out of my room.

Another glorious first.

I've never experienced a girl rushing to get out of my room before. I usually have to drag them out, kicking and screaming, but Mila couldn't leave fast enough.

CHAPTER SEVENTEEN
MILA

What the fuck have I done?

How did I get myself into this mess? How could I have been so stupid, so reckless, so unguarded to allow this to happen?

I don't think twice as I wrap his satin sheets around my naked body, his manly scent encasing me and consuming my senses, keeping me connected to all things dark and dangerous.

As soon as I've found my footing, I rush out of his room, keeping my eyes straight ahead, refusing to look at him.

Shame trickles down my spine as a rush of nausea cripples my stomach, reminding me of my stupid and reckless mistake. A delicious and beautiful, but a disastrous mistake all the same.

Never, not even in my wildest dreams did I ever think last night would lead to me spending the night with Greenmount's very own fuck boy. On my first night on campus, little old me was the one who landed in his bed, even after promising myself that I'd stay far, far away from him.

I cannot believe I even went there.

I told myself over and over again that he was bad news. I have no business—no business whatsoever getting involved with him. Not unless I have a death wish.

I don't know the guy, although I'm now fully acquainted with his anatomy, but what I do know is that he's bad news. He's dangerous and he sure as hell isn't good for me or my health.

I remember being mad. I was so pissed on my drive back to Greenmount after bumping into Cole and his latest squeeze in Frankie's. I was desperate to get out of there and I was scared. All shook up when the storm hit while I was driving. As if things couldn't get any worse, the power cut, a total black out when I pulled up to the apartment and killed the engine.

I was a mess.

I was at my most vulnerable, and what did Jett do? He took advantage of the situation and made his move. It really wouldn't have surprised me if he'd spent the day planning it, perfecting his move right down to finest detail before executing his plan when I stumbled through the door.

The power cut must have been a real added bonus for him too.

Okay, I'll admit that's not the whole truth.

I'd love nothing more than to be able to blame Jett for the whole ordeal, but I actually have a conscience and I know that wouldn't be right, or fair.

The truth is, in the heat of the moment last night, I wanted Jett just as much as he wanted me—if not more. If I'm looking to place the blame then I think I need to start looking closer to home.

Last night was insane. I'd stupidly succumbed to a wild and uncontrollable moment of weakness. There's no doubt in my mind that I should have been stronger. I should have stayed clear of him, but what's done is done. As much as I wish I could, no one holds the power to change the past, so it's pointless me trying to punish myself.

On the plus side, if there's anything good to come out of this mess then its Skye's inevitable reaction. She would be super impressed with me right now. Like she's always told me, the best way to get over a guy is to slide straight beneath the next one. Were her wonderful words of wisdom correct? I guess only time will tell.

And then there's Cole to contend with. My jerk of an ex-boyfriend, rocking up at Frankie's like he has something to prove. He thought it would be cool to turn up to my place of work, knowing full well I'd be there because I'd told him earlier, with some little desperate whore hanging off his arm and no doubt every bullshit word which falls from his mouth.

Well, she's welcome to him. Me and Cole are done. Finished. Never to be repeated ever again.

I know Cole is the least of my worries right now. I have much bigger problems to contend with seeing how I just spent the night with Greenmount's very own glorified fuckboy and I feel disgusted in myself. Total disappointment in my serious lack of judgement. My self-respect went straight out the window and I have no way of getting it back.

I hate myself for being so weak, but I also hate myself because as much as I'd rather burn in hell than admit this out loud, the truth is last night—my forbidden night of sin—was out of this world. It was amazing. My whole body is still on fire from the heat of Jett's' touch. My skin tingles just thinking about how he claimed and possessed me. He took complete control and his hands, mouth, and the rest of his body didn't leave an inch of me untouched.

It's no wonder the girls around here fall at his feet, desperate to capture his attention. No wonder he has them hot on his heels, following him everywhere he goes.

I'm quick to remind myself that I'm nothing like those girls. I have my own mind. I'm not a desperate brainwashed groupie, hoping and praying to be his chosen one for the night. I've never thrown myself at a guy, and I don't have any intention of starting now. I just happened to be in the wrong place at the wrong time, and now I need to find a way to make sure that doesn't happen again.

My brain is being logical here, proving against all odds that it still functions, reminding me that nothing good can ever come from the likes of Jett Jameson; but my body, my foolish body is still crying out, starved of his wicked touch already.

I already know without thinking on it all too much that I've tripped and fallen straight down the rabbit hole. All I can do is hope and pray that I'm strong enough to climb back out before I crumble under his heated touch and reach the point of no return.

The chances are small, growing slimmer by the second, but maybe it's not too late to save myself.

I have to factor in that I'm going to be seeing a whole lot more of Jett than I initially thought, because in a cruel twist of fate, it turns out that the girl on her knees yesterday sucking on Jett like he was the last popsicle, isn't my new roomie after all. I offer up a silent prayer for small mercies, thankful I won't have to face her. Then on the flip side I have to accept that it is in fact Jett who's my new roomie and now I'm forced to live with him for the next nine months. I'm not naive enough to believe I'll be able to avoid him forever but I'm living in hope that there's still a chance. No matter how small.

I was foolish.

I allowed my body to betray me during a crazy moment of madness. I know I shouldn't have succumbed to his wicked and sinful advances, but trust me, in the heat of the moment, Jett is unbelievably hard to say no to. My head was a mess. My emotions were out of whack, totally all over the place.

It's no excuse but Cole had pissed me off. I'd allowed the arrogant son of a bitch into my energy. I'd given him free access to get deep under my skin and no matter how hard I tried; I just couldn't find a way to shake him. I shouldn't have been surprised, but the fact he moved on so fast, so easily, it hurt a whole lot more than I thought it would. I don't know what hurts more, that or the fact he was more than happy to rub it in my face.

In a moment of madness, I'd decided to give myself willingly to Jett, a sure way to play Cole at his own sick and twisted games. Only now I don't feel like a winner. It sounded like a good idea at the time, obviously, but now that I can think with a clear mind all I've gone and done is ruin my fresh start before it's even had a chance to begin.

Way to go Mila.

I catch a glimpse of my reflection in the mirror as I find enough courage to step out of Jett's satin sheets and see my cheeks are still flushed. My hazel eyes shimmer, dancing in the light, displaying sparkles which have never been there before.

What has this dark and dangerous creature done to me?

Climbing into the shower, I throw my head back and embrace the hot jets of water as it runs down my body, slowly removing all traces of Jett and my sinful night, but it's proving to be a hard task.

My mind is on overdrive as a rush of vivid images flow around on repeat, reminding me of the brooding Adonis in the other room, and all the deliciously beautiful things he did to my body; damaging me for anyone else who comes after him.

I can still feel the savage heat of his touch on my body. The intense weight of his hungry lips on mine, desperately searching for more. Now, I'm not the most experienced when it comes to my body or boys for that matter, but Jett, he did things to me that I could only dream of.

He's unstoppable.

He's insatiable.

And I have zero business getting involved with the devil. This, whatever it may be, it needs to end and it needs to end now. Me and Jett cannot become fuck buddies. Hell, it sure looks like he has enough of them to go around, anyways.

I try to shift my mindset and instead focus on washing my hair and scrubbing my body, but I can still feel him all over me, continuing to consume every fiber of my being... claiming me for all eternity.

A part of me hates that I can't shut him out, but another unstable, wicked part of me loves what he's done to me. No wonder these girls go wild for him if this is the effect he has on them.

I continue to wash away my sins but it's no good. It's pointless as I quickly come to the harsh realization that no matter how hard I scrub, how hard I try to wash him away, Jett has done the unthinkable. He's imprinted himself on me. He's left a permanent mark, a reminder of our night together, and I'll never be able to rid myself of him, or the memory.

Shutting off the shower, I step out, eager to get dried, dressed and escape the claustrophobic confines of this apartment, and Jett, if only for a little while.

He's older than me so I'm hopeful our paths won't cross during the school day. I'm praying those few hours of freedom will allow me time to collect my thoughts and come up with some kind of epic plan... a plan either to avoid him or find a way to talk to him. Adult to adult, figuring out a way together to move past our mistake so our living arrangements don't become awkward.

I don't like it, and the thought of Jett watching my every move fills me with a deep sense of dread, but I'm prepared to do whatever I need to do to keep my place here. Going back to my mom's is not an option. Not now... not ever.

I realize my mistake instantly. In my urgent rush to escape Jett's room and his predatorial glare I completely forgot to scoop up my clothes, and I didn't rush to my room. One because I'm not even sure which one is mine, and two; my belongings are still downstairs, exactly where I left them yesterday, in the middle of the hallway.

Way to go Mila. You sure know how to fuck things up for yourself, don't you?

What am I supposed to do now? I look around the bathroom and find nothing that I need. There's not a single towel in here and by the looks of things I'm going to have to walk out of here butt naked, and the universe will obviously make it so I bump into Jett.

Refusing to believe I'm out of options, I rummage through the cupboards, also finding them empty. I come up blank... slowly accepting my fate when I find a scrunched up blue top hiding in the corner.

I throw up a silent prayer of thanks while hoping the top isn't dirty. Beggars can't be choosers and all that. It will have to do. It's not for long. All I need is a little cover, trying to preserve the small ounce of modesty I have left, so I can run across the hall, down the stairs to grab my belongings and then back upstairs to find my room. It's not too much to ask for, is it?

I set my plan in motion and quickly pat myself dry before sliding my arms into the Jersey, quickly discovering that said item of clothing belongs to the very person I'm trying to avoid. I see *Jameson* embroidered on the back, followed by the number 8 underneath, and I inwardly groan.

Sure, this isn't the best idea I've ever had, but when all's said and done, what choice do I have, really?

My knees become weak and almost buckle under the weight of my small frame the moment Jett's manly scent invades my senses; his Cedarwood smell like a crisp autumn morning clings to my skin, consuming me like I didn't even bother to wash him away. The fabric is ultra soft against my bare flesh, causing a multitude of goose pimples to break out across my skin and I know it has nothing to do with the drop in temperature.

I just can't seem to catch a break from him.

Shaking my hair out, it falls in damp waves across my face and when I turn to the mirror I almost jump out of my skin when I find Jett standing behind me, his large muscular frame towering over me, making me feel even smaller than before.

My blood runs cold. My heart somersaults in my chest, before stopping completely when I recognize the savage hunger in his deep jade green eyes. My mind is screaming at me to stay away from him, but my body has other ideas, intent on betraying me as my breath catches in my throat.

'I'm sorry...' I stammer out, slowly turning around to face him and his green eyes blaze with thunder. Wrong move. Wrong fucking move. So, the guy has no problem sharing a bed with me, but there must be an invisible line when it comes to borrowing an item of his clothing. Even if it is to shield my modesty. 'I couldn't find anything else to wear.' It sounds like a lame ass excuse but it's nothing but the truth.

Jett doesn't say anything and a heavy blanket of silence falls around us. He doesn't move. He doesn't make a sound as he continues to burn me with his heated look, drinking me in like he didn't get enough of me last night.

Finally, after what feels like a lifetime of silence passing between us, Jett takes one last stride toward me and closes the small distance between us. His broad muscular chest rises and falls rapidly, contradicting his hardened exterior. I can see that I'm affecting him just as much as he's affecting me. A small gasp escapes me when he reaches out and cups my chin between his thumb and forefinger, forcing me to look directly at him... and only him.

'My number looks good on you, princess.' He growls out and before I have a chance to think, to move, to focus on my surroundings, his soft warm, dominating lips come crashing down against mine, claiming me as his own once again.

I can't breathe. My heart accelerates in my chest as his big warm hands slide under his Jersey and grip my waist.

I need to stop this. I shouldn't want him, but he captivates me, pulling me in until I'm consumed by all things Jett Jameson.

I feel his mouth curving at the edges as he whispers, 'but you'd look so much better out of it.'

I ignore my mind, refusing to listen to my ego screaming out at me to be careful, warning me to stay as far away as physically possible from this dangerous beast before me. Once again, I shut it out and instead allow my body to lead even though I know I'll live to regret it later.

I don't even think as my hands move freely on their own accord as they slide up his broad back and I feel the pull of his muscles tense from the contact. They keep moving up, and I choose to memorize the feeling, saving it away, securing a so I can come back at a later date. So, I can torture myself some more.

A small groan escapes his lips as my hands come to a stop at the base of his neck, my fingers instantly finding a safe space in his messy damp black curls.

This time, I'm the one who takes control as I reach up on my tip toes, pressing my hungry lips harder against his.

My heart is skyrocketing in my chest, and no matter how hard I push myself against him it's not enough. It will never be enough.

I allow myself to lose all inhibitions, succumbing to his touch, my mind, body and soul suddenly dependent on him ... Jett is fast becoming my life source.

'Beg for me, princess.' Jett moans into my mouth, his voice as soft as melted butter. 'Tell me how much you want me.'

'Jett...' I whisper breathlessly. It's all I manage as my head spins, lost in the moment as his big warm hand slides up my thigh, moving closer to the apex and another rush of desire builds at my core. I'm aware that I'm about to willingly allow another mistake to happen...

Almost...

Until a loud knock on the front door sounds out around us, quickly bringing me back to my senses.

'Ignore it.' Jett orders on a growl, his voice firm as I try to pull away from his heated embrace. Jett, however, seems to be in no rush to move. His eyes lock onto mine, holding me in place as his hand continues to tantalizingly work its way between my heated thighs. My body is blazing with desire, tingling from head to toe when his expert finger slides against my weak spot, stroking softly at first, before gliding deep inside me, thrusting in and out and I almost buckle under his touch.

The knock sounds again. Louder this time and I know that this is a sign. The universe's way of telling me to back the hell up and stay away from him.

No matter how good this feels right now, in the moment, the pleasure will never compare to the inevitable pain I'm going to feel when this silly illusion breaks and shatters down around me.

This is my final warning.

CHAPTER EIGHTEEN
MILA

'Leave it.' Jett growls out again. 'Whoever it is can wait.' He moans around his distracting and intoxicating kiss, but deep inside my mind I'm adamant this is my cue to up and leave.

It pains me to break away from him and at first, I don't think I'm strong enough, but somehow, against all odds I find the strength to pull back. When I look at him his eyes are wide with shock, swimming with disbelief that I could think about pulling away from him, let alone actually do it.

I've disabled him momentarily and I choose this moment, my sudden unexpected advantage and dart around Jett's large frame before rushing out of the bathroom.

It's not lost on me that this is the second time I have ran away from him and his advances this morning.

As I rush through the apartment, I'm beyond thankful to find it empty. Just me and Jett like I'd initially thought. The last thing I need is to be running headfirst into Sienna after spending the night and most of this morning with Jett.

I have no idea what's happening between them, but they seem to hate each other with a passion. A small part of me wonders if he did her dirty in the past and she still holds a grudge.

The knock sounds out again, and I'm grateful to whoever is standing on the other side of the door. Grateful because they managed to bring me back to my senses and tear me away from Jett and his deadly charms. I'm clearly no good in the heated presence of Jett Jameson. I cannot be trusted when I'm around him, obviously.

I come to a sudden stop, my boxes still in the same position I left them in yesterday and reach out to open the door. I take in the unwelcome sight before me, instantly regretting every word. I take it all back.

'Cole?' I stammer, the shock echoing around me and evident in my voice. 'What are you doing here?' I demand, my anger quickly playing catch up as a flutter of vivid images of Cole and his new girl crash to the forefront of my mind. I guess he didn't think he'd humiliated me enough last night and now decided to come back for round two.

'Can we talk?'

'Seriously?' I bite back, and my whole-body trembles as the adrenaline starts to kick in. 'I didn't think there was anything left to say.' He flinches but quickly composes himself again, in only the way Cole can. 'Your words, not mine.' I remind him on the off chance he's forgotten.

I push the door, ready to slam it shut on his arrogant face, but Cole has other ideas. As usual he's one hundred percent prepared for my retaliation. His foot is already inside the door, preventing me from closing it. Well, I could always slam it and hopefully break his foot in the process.

His beloved hockey season would be over before it even had a chance to begin.

'Mila... please...'

'Go home Cole.' My voice is stern and I barely recognize myself. 'I have nothing left to say to you.'

His eyes, solely focused on me just moments before, veer off slightly and lock on to something else. I watch as his face floods with disbelief and his cold empty black eyes grow wide with shock. It's in this moment I quickly realize what his problem is. I'm standing before him wearing nothing but Jett's Jersey. A Jersey which only just about covers my body.

'Wait...' he throws a hand up as he barks. 'What the fuck are you wearing?' Fury blazes in his eyes and I don't think I have ever witnessed him so mad before. 'Is that another jock's Jersey on your back?'

Before I have time to answer, Jett suddenly appears behind me, no doubt half naked and looking as deadly as ever. I don't even falter when I feel the heat of his hand gripping my hip, his other one slowly snaking it's way around my waist as he pulls my body flush against his.

Cole looks murderous and I hear a soft chuckle rumbling deep within Jett's chest as he snarls, 'See that...' Jett presses his palm flush against my stomach, gripping the fabric so his Jersey inches higher. 'Thats my number she's wearing. Mila belongs to me now.'

'Less than five minutes ago I couldn't wait to escape the unbearable heat of Jett Jameson, yet now, as I stand here glaring down my ex, shielded under his protective touch, whilst being reminded what those sinful fingers can do, I don't want to be anywhere else and an unstoppable sense of power creeps in and takes hold of me.

Cole might have fooled himself into thinking he had one over on me last night, but when I watch the defeat taking over his face right now, I know it's me who holds the ace card. Obviously, his side piece wasn't all that, and now he's out of options, Cole has decided to crawl back to me.

Desperately begging me to take him back, only his plan has well and truly backfired. Instead of trying to win me back, he's tracked me down, only to find me flushed and content in someone else's arms.

'If I remember correctly, last night you told me you'd already moved on, and I should think about doing the same.' I raise a brow, daring him to argue with me. 'Looks like I decided to take your advice.'

'Mila...'

'Goodbye Cole.'

'This isn't over.' He warns, but that's all I hear when Jett reaches over me and slams the door in his startled and unsuspecting face.

'Good riddance to bad news.'

CHAPTER NINETEEN
JETT

'Do you wanna tell me what that was about?' Mila demands as soon as she's caught her breath and her small button nose wrinkles in disgust as she glares at me.

I hold my hands up in fake surrender, not seeing any kind of problem. 'What, did you want to stand there and speak to him?' I question, already knowing what her answer will be.

I wait patiently as her small, yet mighty frame slowly moves toward me, her damp honey blonde hair falling in natural waves at her shoulders, and her stormy hazel eyes are wide with fury. She looks hella cute when she's worked up, but I'm wise enough to keep my mouth closed for once. As much as I'd love to retaliate, I value my balls and any minute now this little pocket rocket is about to explode.

Eventually her mouth, that perfect delicious little mouth opens in protest. 'Whether I want to talk to him or not is none of your concern.' She hisses back at me, and the venom on her tongue is potent. 'Believe it or not, I survived long enough without you. I don't need you to fight my battles.'

'I don't doubt it. 'A ghost of a smile plays on my lips. This chick is a feisty one for sure, and I am so here for it. I'm not used to girls arguing with me. I'm not used to them questioning me. I'm used to them doing anything they can to please me. But Mila... this chick does whatever the hell she wants, zero fucks given, and it sure makes for a welcome and refreshing change.

She's unapologetic.

I'm not sure what she's done to me, but I'm more than willing to find out.

'Maybe you should take a step back and allow me to fight them, then.' She hurts back at me trying to stand tall and hold her ground. Her dark brows furrow as she takes me in, stepping closer. She places both of her hands palm down on my chest, in turn sending an unexpected jolt of electricity through me, coursing through my veins and I know she feels it too.

'My dick was inside you less than twelve hours ago...'

'And?' Her voice is like a whip slashing across my skin, and I can feel the heat of my anger as my nostril's flare.

'And...' I bite out, unable to stop myself and I grip her chin between my thumb and forefinger, squeezing harder than necessary so she's forced to look at me, 'Whether you like it or not, that means you belong to me now.' My jaw sets and I feel the vein at my temple throbbing violently, giving away my true emotions.

What the fuck has she done to me?

I'm Jett Jameson. A one-man band. I don't limit myself to one chick. I never have and I'm not about to start now. My mind is all out of whack, but one thing I'm certain of, now that I've touched her, now that I've had a taste I'll make sure no other guy goes near her.

I meant what I said... every fucking word. Mila Daniels is mine now and there's not a goddamn thing she can do to change it. 'You make me sick,' she stammers when the shock of my confession has subsided and she finds her voice again. 'I'm glad, but I could say the same for you.' When she narrows her eyes in confusion, I add, 'Cole Williams?' I raise a curious brow at her, trying to understand the attraction, but as usual with Mila I quickly slam headfirst into a brick wall and come up blank.

'You know him?' She sounds shocked, totally caught off guard. Usually this would be the perfect opportunity to play a few mind games, but for once in my life I see no reason to lie to her.

Another first.

'You could say that?' Now I have her full attention, I'm desperate to keep it.

'How? Cole goes to Ravendale, not Greenmount.'

I can't help but laugh at her own naivety. 'He's the captain of the Raven's, right?'

'Yeah... but I'm still not following. What does his position have to do with you?' confusion dances onto her petite face and it takes everything I have to stop myself from reaching out and claiming her once more in only the way I can.

'I don't think I had time to introduce myself properly to you since we met.' A notorious grin snakes onto my lips knowing my next words will either destroy her or make her want me more.

'What aren't you telling me?'

'Allow me to introduce you to the captain of the Greenmount Giants.' It takes a minute for my words to sink in. 'I'm your ex's biggest rival on the ice, and now it looks like I just levelled up on the personal front, too.'

'No, no, no...' she shakes her head, refusing to believe what I've just told her. 'This cannot be happening. I already told you last night shouldn't have happened...'

'Ah, but it did, princess. 'I laugh.

'Quit calling me that,' she snaps and her cheeks grow bright crimson. Obviously little miss smart mouth didn't expect our lives to line up so perfectly. To be fair, neither did I, but I'm not the one front and center in denial right now.

'and...' I continue, refusing to give her despair any airtime, if your asshat of an ex hadn't turned up, trying to hammer down the door like the sore loser he really is, I'm willing to bet everything I have that I'd be balls deep inside that sweet little pussy of yours right now.'

She swallows down hard, trying to think of her next move, but she's not going anywhere. I have her right where I want her and she sure as hell knows it too.

'Full of yourself, much?' She retorts but her uneven voice lets me know that I've done my job. I've gotten to her and her composure is slipping. 'Let's just hope you burned it to memory because I promise right now that a repeat won't ever be happening again.'

'I wouldn't flatter yourself, princess.' I slowly run my forefinger down her jaw, along her neck before stopping just above her pert breasts and her whole body shakes from my touch. 'I was down for a good time, not a lifetime.'

'Wow. Has anyone ever told you you're a grade A Jerk?' She hurls, refusing to back down while trying her damned hardest to get to me, but if anything, I find her dramatic little outburst comical.

'Oh, I know... but you'll never find me apologizing for it.'

Mila narrows her eyes at me, a mixture of hunger and disgust before trying to shove her way past me, but I hold her back with ease. No way am I about to let her escape for the third time.

'Get your hands off me.' She shouts. 'Let me go.'

'No one can hear you. it's just you and me, princess.' sickeningly that thought excites me.

'I mean it Jett, get off me.'

I cock my head to the side, trying to get a better read on her. 'From memory that's not what you were saying last night.'

'I'm not playing games, Jett. Forget last night and let me go.' I find it cute that she's still trying to hold her own, standing her ground against my large frame, but I can already tell that she's never come across someone like me before.

Cole Williams, that son of a bitch is a pussy compared to me, and if Mila doesn't back the fuck down, she'll end up learning that the hard way.

'Thats the problem. I can't forget last night and neither can you.'

'You don't know the first thing about me.'

'You'd be surprised.' A sigh of defeat rolls from her shoulders as she quickly realizes she isn't going to escape me until she decides to play this game by my rules.

'What do you want from me?'

Running my hand along my jaw, I reward her with a victorious grin. 'Actually, now that you mention it, I could use a favor.'

'Why should I do anything for you?' She hisses, the venom rolling freely from her tongue.

'Because you owe me...'

'I don't owe you shit.'

Really?' I question, waiting for her to catch up. 'Pretty sure I just got that waste of space off your back.'

'I can handle Cole myself.'

'Sure looked like it from where I was standing.' Her eyes narrow some more and my dick stirs to life, as though she's just gripped me at the base and pumped blood back into it.

'I don't owe you anything.' She repeats, more to convince herself than me.

'Oh, Princess... I'm afraid you do and now I'm here to collect.' Mila quickly realizes she's not about to win this fight, instantly backing down before she says on a heated whisper. 'What do you want from me?'

'Now we're talking.' I offer her a wink which in turn wins me no favors. 'There's a game happening this Saturday...'

'A game? What kind of game?'

'A game...' What the hell doesn't she understand about that.

'Yeah, I heard you,' she argues back with me, her hands falling and landing on her small hips. 'Maybe you could be more specific... spin the bottle... football?'

'Football?' I exclaim? 'I just told you I'm the Captain of the Giants, and you ask if it's football?' I can't stop the laugh which rumbles from deep within my chest. Either she's playing with me, or she's genuinely that naive. 'Plus, if spin the bottle was the game then it would have been game over for you last night.' I smile, a deep sense of victory coursing through me when she flinches at my words, and most likely the memory. 'No, the Giants have a game, and it's a big game.'

'I don't understand why you'd need a favor from me... unless you're expecting me to fill your position?' The sarcasm falls freely from her tongue and it's like looking at a female version of myself.

'I'd like you to be there.' I struggle to say the words. This is the first time I've ever invited anyone to come watch me play. There are heaps of girls out in the stands cheering me on, but this is the first time I've actually wanted someone there and I'm not all too sure how I feel about it.

'Hate to break it to you, but hockey isn't my thing.'

'Bullshit.' I fire back. 'I just found out you were dating the Raven's captain and you expect me to believe that hockey isn't your thing?' Puck bunnies go wild for all things hockey, and Mila shouldn't be any different, but something is telling me this chick is all kinds of different. Maybe that's the attraction.

'Exactly... Cole is the main reason why hockey isn't my thing.' She deadpans and I'm happy that she utters his name with so much distaste.

'Look, it doesn't have to be your thing.' I say, trying my damned hardest to convince her in this. I'm fucking pleading the fifth here. Another first. 'I'll be honest with you. It's a big game and although it might not sound true, but I really struggle to focus, to concentrate when all those crazy puck bunnies make a run for me.'

Mila shakes her head, not sure she heard me right but she sets her jaw, her hazel eyes blazing into me, holding me captive as I wait for her response. 'Well, that sure sounds like a you problem from where I'm standing.'

'Sure it is,' I confess. 'And I'm usually happy to own it, but you owe me, remember. Now I'm making it your problem too.'

She thinks on my words for a moment, her hands still placed on my chest and I struggle to push her away. 'What's in it for me?'

'Plenty.' I step closer to her, backing her against the wall. 'All you have to do is pretend to be with me. Act like you're my girlfriend and I promise it will be a win-win for both of us.' When she looks at me like I've just grown two heads, I say, 'I'll be able to concentrate on the game and soon enough word will travel back to Ravendale and dickweed that you now belong to the Captain of the Giants. He'll leave you alone in no time.'

'I don't belong to anyone.'

Bringing my face closer to hers, I close my eyes and breathe her in. 'Allow me to let you in on a little secret, princess. I'm the King of this town and if I say I own someone then you can bet your ass that I fucking own them.'

I watch her mull the idea over in her mind and I'm pleased when she doesn't outright tell me no. Instead, she moves even closer to me and I can feel the blazing heat of her skin through my jersey, and it's fucking torture knowing that I could take her at any second. But I'm trying to play nicely here. I need to get her on side if my plan is going to work.

'Get out of my way and I'll think about it. How's that sound?'

Checkmate.

Mila flashes me an award-winning smile as I reluctantly step back and for the first time in my life, I'm held at the mercy of a fucking girl. My balls might still be attached to my body but this chick, she's got them right in the palm of her hands and she sure as hell knows it too.

I'm screwed.

Well and truly fucked, and I have no idea how I'm going to break free from her captivating spell. Mila Daniels has done what no other girl before her has ever been able to do. She has me hook, line, and sinker, and I don't even hate it.

CHAPTER TWENTY
MILA

My head is still spinning.

I'm still hung up on all things Jett that my first day went by in a blur.

All my classes were a total haze of nothingness. I cannot allow this to happen. I need to have a clear head. I need to be able to focus clearly on my studies. I can't afford to lose my mind to all things Jett Jameson. If I do then it's inevitable that I'll fail my exams and I'll be back in Coldwater living with my mom again faster than I can say shit.

On the plus side, I still haven't bumped into Sienna so I guess that's something. A small silver lining in the darkened cloud of doom hanging over my head. I know I shouldn't get ahead of myself. Especially given that we're roomies, I'm bound to bump into her sooner or later. It's only going to be a matter of time. What am I supposed to do when she's back at the apartment when she's there? You can cut the sexual chemistry between me and Jett with a blunt knife. I haven't known Sienna for long, but it's clear for all to see that her and Jett hate each other with a passion.

Fortunately for me, I have another joyful shift at Frankie's to keep my mind busy, so long as Cole doesn't stroll in with another one of his latest victims. I don't think I can handle another showdown with him so soon after this morning. He's already taken enough energy from me for one day.

My phone buzzes to life as I pull into the parking lot at Frankie's and my heart deflates when I see the caller I.D. I knew it would only be a matter of time before my mom was back on my case. It wouldn't be long before she came out of her stupor, suddenly remembering I exist so she can hound me for her next fix. A small part of me is telling me I should answer it, check that she's okay but I just can't do it. My body no longer holds that kind of energy to be dealing with her never ending drama's alongside everything else I've had going on in the past twenty-four hours.

I try my best not to feel guilty as I allow the call to ring off. I know she'll keep ringing and I'll keep ignoring her. I'm determined to act how I mean to go on and succumbing to defeat won't get me far. I know if anything bad had happened, or if it was urgent then I'd quickly hear about it now that I'm back in Coldwater. Someone at Frankie's would have heard the news, and they'd come rushing to tell me everything they'd heard.

One thing about growing up in a small town is that everyone knows your business, no matter how much of a low profile you keep for yourself. It's a pointless act because they always figure everything out in the end.

'What's poppin' stranger.' Skye is in my face the second I walk through the old wooden doors to Frankie's. Something which seems to be becoming quite the occurrence lately.

'Same day, different shit.' I snap back as I make my way toward the bar to grab my apron. A little blunt, maybe, but if Skye thinks I've forgotten how she tried to play with my emotions yesterday then she really needs to snap out of her little bubble and wake up. 'What's happening with you, or am I not allowed to hear about all the new fun you're having while I'm not around?'

'Oh, come on, Mila.' She pouts back at me. 'If this is about last night...'

'Too right this is about last night.' I know I'm taking all of my frustration out on her, but what did she expect?

'I was just messing with you.' She tries to plead the fifth, desperate to climb out of the large hole she's falling into, but her bullshit isn't washing with me. Not this time. 'I was angry. You'd just upped and left, surely you can understand that?'

I turn to face her as I tie my apron behind my back and I notice that even though she's pouting at me, silently begging for forgiveness, she still has that wicked sparkle in her eyes. 'Sure, I understand you were pissed I left town, but we've already been through this. I told you we'd still see each other, almost daily. What I don't understand is you trying to turn years of friendship into some kind of power trip. I won't be in the middle, Skye. I'm either in or out, so you decide.'

My tone is harsh, but I'm allowed to be angry too. She had her meltdown yesterday and now it's my time. Let's see how she likes the taste of her own medicine. I should probably tone it down a little, but I can't stop myself. Skye is the only person in my life who's always there for me. She knows everything about me. The good, the bad and the nasty. She's the only person I can vent to. The only person who won't judge me... and its wrong. So fucking wrong that by me trying to better myself, it's driven a wedge between us.

Hell, moving out of Coldwater was supposed to be better for me and my soul, and if anything, it seems like I've made all of my problems ten times worse.

'Are you done with your bitch fit?' She demands, her hands splayed on her curvaceous hips letting me know that she means business and my resolve weakens some.

'That all depends.'

'On...?' She asks. I narrow my eyes, trying my damned hardest not to drop my guard first. It's hard when me and Skye have a disagreement. We're two of the same soul. All we want to do is tell each other to stop being stupid and throw our arms around each other, but at the same time we're also both stubborn as hell and neither one of us wants to be the one who backs down first.

'On whether you're over yourself and if you're going to put me back in the loop?'

A megawatt smile breaks out across Skye's face and a wild sense of victory runs through my veins. I knew if I held my composure long enough that she would be the one to break first. Whenever Skye has news, she can't keep it to herself to save her life.

'Well... now that I have your full attention... I might have something to tell you.'

'No shit.' I knew it. Skye is rubbish when it comes to hiding things from me. She's never been able to master the art and now I don't think she ever will. To be honest, I don't know why she keeps trying, yet here we are.

'So, tell me then...' I lean across the bar and swipe my notepad, ready to get straight to work, all ready to take people's orders and keep my mind busy until closing time.

'Okay...' she bites down on her lower lip, worrying it between her teeth. A sure sign if ever there was one that I'm not going to like what she has to say. 'But first I need you to pinkie promise that no matter what I say you won't get mad?' She begins and my anxiety skyrockets through the roof. Maybe I was best off not knowing. At least what I don't know can't hurt me, right? Before either of us has a chance to say anything else, the diner door swings open and my heart stops, dropping straight down into the pit of my stomach.

No... no... no... this cannot be happening.

An all too familiar pair of jade green eyes look right at me and a multitude of foreign emotions ripple through my body. My knees go weak and if I wasn't leaning on the bar then I'm sure I'd be on my ass right now. No one else seems to see the despair taking over my body. I'm frozen, rooted in place while watching my nightmare slowly unfold before my eyes.

What the hell is Jett Jameson doing in Coldwater? He's from Greenmount U. We both know he has no business driving into Coldwater and taking residence at Frankie's.

Has he followed me? A small icy shudder runs down my spine when I think about that possibility. Is he taking this whole fake girlfriend thing seriously? I thought he just wanted me to rock up to his game on Saturday and that would be the end of it.

This has to be another one of his messed-up mind games. I make a mental note not to fall for his bullshit and instead focus on keeping my head held high. Skye cannot find out what happened between us last night. Not now... not ever.

Jett Jameson is going to be a secret I'll need to take to the grave with me. She also can't hear it from someone else either. If she's going to find out then I need to make sure that I'm the one who tells her... and I'll only ever tell her when the time is right.

'I've met someone...' Skye's voice cuts through my thoughts and I barely hear her. 'I've met someone, Mila.' She tells me again, louder this time. 'That date I was teasing you about, well I wanted to tell you to your face and I thought what better way to do that than introduce the two of you.'

Seriously?

Everything slowly falls into place and I feel sick. Mentally and physically. My eyes grow wide and I can't even describe the anger I feel as it wreaks havoc and rushes through my body, like wildfire. I can't speak. My throat constricts as I try to swallow down hard on the lump of emotion which has formed there.

I don't even know why I'm surprised. I knew Jett Jameson was a seasoned fuck boy and I'm the unwilling victim who fell into his trap. I'll always own my mistakes, but to make a move on my best friend. That's a whole other level of fucked up. A level I'm not even prepared to deal with.

I slowly cast my eyes between Jett and Skye and my heart stammers deep in my chest. My breathing comes in short, fast bursts and I feel any second now I'm about to start hyperventilating. This can't be happening. This has to be some kind of sick and twisted joke.

I snap my eyes back toward my best friend and growl, 'you're screwing a Giant?' I hiss, unable to keep the venom out of my voice. It doesn't help my composure when I sense Jett watching me closely in my peripheral and all the small hairs on the back of my neck stand tall... confirmation that I should have listened to my gut and stayed clear of him.

He's bad news.

He's dangerous.

Jett Jameson is all kinds of wrong but no matter what I do, I just can't seem to stay away from him.

He's everywhere I look.

He's everywhere I turn... like he's dead set on tormenting and torturing me for the rest of my living days. I can't even come to Coldwater to escape him. I force myself to look up at him through my lashes to see if he's making his way over to the bar, and sure enough he is. He oozes confidence just like I knew he would but he's cautious in his step all the same.

Skye is fucking a Giant... and not just any Giant, but *my Giant*. I shake my head, quickly reminding myself that I'm being stupid. Jett Jameson isn't mine. That guy isn't anyone's. Like he told me, he's here for a good time, not a lifetime. Just because he asked me to be his fake girlfriend, a favor for him not me, that doesn't mean shit. Has anyone ever been exclusive when they've been fake dating? I highly doubt it. How could I have been so stupid? So gullible? So goddamn naive.

Obviously, I'm only good enough for when the moment suits. When he needs to use me so he can keep the rest of the female population at bay. But it sure looks like that deal was short-lived and he's replaced me already... with none other than my best friend.

'Not just any Giant...' Skye beams next to me, her eyes glowing like all her Christmases have come at once. A deep rush of nausea sweeps over me as Jett comes and stands between us. His fuck girls. And I don't mistake the evil glint in his eye. This motherfucker has played me and he's played me good. I bet this son of a bitch is loving every fucking moment of this. Again, I shouldn't be all too surprised because this is what fuck boys do. They play girls against each other to boost their own ego's, not giving a damn about any lasting damage on the victims who are left behind.

'I'll take a cherry coke and whatever you're having, princess.' His voice is as smooth as velvet to my ears and when I look at him all I can see is his beautiful mouth, a mouth which brought my whole body alive, and no doubt Skye's too.

'I told you, my name isn't princess, it's Mila.'

I bite back, my voice as cold as ice for a moment and he looks taken aback. His darkened brow creases in confusion, all traces of humor vanishing from his angular face. This guy can try to fool me all he likes, but I'm so much smarter than he's willing to give me credit for.

'And I told you, princess stays.'

'Woah, did I miss something here?' Skye cuts in and I suddenly remember it's not just me and Jett in the room, the way it was back in our apartment.

The thought of Skye and Jett together has my stomach in knots, and I'm in no mood to play anyone's games. 'I don't know...' I reply curtly. 'Did you?' I turn to look at my best friend and find her watching Jett like a hawk, drinking him up like she can't get enough of him. It's sickening and a little soul destroying too. Unable to help myself, I elbow her in the side, desperate to tear her attention away from him. 'I thought you were supposed to have better taste.'

My blood is at boiling point and it's not lost on me that I'm acting like a spoiled, self-entitled brat, but right in this moment I don't really care.

How can Jett hook up with my best friend and then seduce me at the same time? I know he's a glorified fuck boy and that's what's expected of him, but there are levels. It's not like Jett doesn't know who she is because Skye was at the Lake party with me and I'm pretty sure she made a lasting impression.

He saw her with me and he still went out of his way to play us both. How am I supposed to break something like this to Skye?

'Baby...' A deep voice booms out from behind Jett. A voice I don't recognize. 'I'm sorry I'm late,' he pants breathlessly. When Jett moves to the side, his friend who was also at the lake party comes into view and the whole diner falls silent, their attention firmly focused on the four of us at the bar. The new guy doesn't even look at me, instead he nods once at Jett before focusing all his attention on Skye. It's like this guy doesn't see anyone else but her as he moves toward her. I watch, my mouth open wide with shock as the scene unfolds before me. He doesn't falter, regardless of everyone around us watching as he takes her into his arms, and it's in this moment I realize I fucked up, majorly.

I got this situation so wrong and, in the process, through my own error of judgment I've foolishly allowed my feelings to show. Feelings I've been trying to hide ever since I first laid my eyes on his ruggedly beautiful face and I know he hasn't missed it either. Me and my big fucking mouth. Always jumping to conclusions without trying to learn the facts first.

I fucked up and I fucked up big.

It shouldn't matter. I shouldn't care who Jett does or doesn't fuck. That's his prerogative—but I'll always draw the line when it comes to my best friend.

I can also try to kid myself until my last breath, but I know the real reason why I acted out, and that's because deep down in my heart of hearts I want Jett. I want him more than I've ever wanted anyone else in my life. And what pains me the most, what makes me just as sad as the rest of his desperate groupies, I want Jett to want me just as much. I want him to feel the same.

Hell, I need him to feel the same.

Not that anyone will ever hear me admit that fact out loud. My feelings will be something else I'll be taking to the grave with me.

Jett Jameson wasn't put on this earth to give someone their happy-ever-after. No, he was placed here by the devil himself so he can torture them and drag them straight to hell.

CHAPTER TWENTY-ONE
JETT

It's game day, and I am so fucking ready for it.

My veins are alive, thrumming with electricity and the static pumps and it energizes my heart, gearing me up for the epic events of today.

Give me any girl and I'll easily make her day or night, but this... this adrenaline is what being a Giant is all about. I live and breathe ice hockey. To feel the ice as my boots mercilessly glide over it, it's liberating and I'm a force to be reckoned with.

No one has been able to take me down yet.

I'm untouchable, undefeated, and that's how it will always stay.

I spend most of my time practicing. I practice like there's no tomorrow because I have to be on top of my game. There's zero room for distraction. The game... the sweat... the tears... that's what dreams are fucking made of, and I have no intention of losing this feeling. I have no intentions of stopping—ever—not while there's air in my lungs and blood in my veins.

I'd be lying If I said this week hadn't been a shit show at best and this game is just what I need to restart my mind. To kick me back into reality and fast. Everything and I mean everything has been up in the air, but I always feel so much better, more at ease when I've been out on the ice.

It speaks to my soul and reminds me of my main purpose in this life. I was born to play and I'm hoping for more of the same when I put these jerks on their asses today.

I find Sienna and Mila both head down in the kitchen when I stroll through the door. Sienna is busy checking her socials, as per fucking usual, and Mila is nose deep in her studies. I never imagined she'd be the geeky type, but then she's been full of surprises so far. It doesn't escape my attention that the two of them couldn't be any different and it baffles me. It totally blows my mind how they've managed to strike up a friendship in such a short space of time. Maybe that's because I've never been open to allowing strangers into my personal space, into my mind on a personal level, but Sienna has always been an open book.

It takes me a minute, but I eventually walk over to them, neither of them noticing my presence and without thinking I reach out and swipe the textbook from under Mila's nose. Dickish move, maybe, but it doesn't sit right with me that her attention didn't jump straight to me when I walked into the room. Childish, maybe.

'What the hell do you think you're doing?' She demands when she looks up at me and her hazel eyes are ablaze with a mixture of anger and embarrassment. She looks hella cute but I feel zero remorse. Mila might hold the power to bring out a whole lot of firsts in me, but the sick and twisted Jett Jameson is still hidden deep within me, showing no signs of being removed completely.

'I'm doing you a favor and bringing you back to the land of the living.' I cast my eyes down at the textbook she's currently working on and see that her English Lit is as cliche as ever. Romeo and Juliet? 'No one around here studies on Saturdays.' I confirm and she glowers back at me, clearly in no mood to play my games. I don't let that deter me though. I'm Jett Jameson and when I want something I'll always make sure I get it. No matter the cost.

In an instant, Mila is out of her seat and she's jumping up and down before me like some kind of feral savage dog, desperate to retrieve her textbook out of my hands. I laugh and throw my head back when she reaches out and raises her arm high above her head, and we both know there's no way she'll be able to reach me. Mila will never be able to get the book out of my hand. As she jumps up and down some more, I decide to use this time wisely and I take a moment to appreciate the curve of her breasts as they almost fall out of her camisole, and I sure as hell ain't complaining.

Hell, I could stay here all day doing this and I wouldn't get bored. The truth is I don't think I could ever get bored with Mila and her smart-ass mouth around, period.

'Give me that back...' she shouts and her cheeks flush deep crimson, a sure sign of her anger.

'Jett, quit being a dick and leave her alone.' Sienna chimes in and I don't know whether to be happy she's finally sticking up for someone other than herself, or to be pissed that she's not on my side. 'She's not harming anyone.'

'I think it's best if you stay out of this, Cee...' I warn, not that Sienna has ever listened to me before.

'Give it back.' Mila shouts again and I hate to admit it but I am so here for this cat and mouse chase we seem to have going on.

'How much do you want it?' I ask and I know she doesn't miss the double meaning in my question. I just can't seem to stop myself from teasing her, desperate to get some kind of reaction from her, no matter how small. Mila is fast becoming my new addiction and no matter how hard I try; I just can't seem to wean myself away from her.

'I'm not playing your games.'

'Pity...' I laugh back. 'Just when I was feeling sorry for you and about to give it back. Maybe I'll hold onto it for a while longer?' I pause, watching how her breathing is coming in quick short bursts and I know I still have a wild effect on her, the same as she does me. 'Unless...'

'Unless what?' She huffs back, while rolling her eyes dramatically and it takes everything I have to hold back and stop myself from giving her something to roll her eyes at.

'Have you thought about coming to the game with me later?' I keep my voice light, trying not to make it sound like a big deal, but we all know it is. Mila hasn't mentioned my proposition since and I need to know if we have a deal. I know she hasn't forgotten what's on offer. I know she hasn't forgotten what I've asked of her. She's just been a stubborn bitch and refusing to acknowledge it out loud.

The moment the words left my lips I instantly feel the heat of Sienna's eyes burning into me, but as usual I decide to ignore her, shutting her out is second nature to me. It's like an automatic response. I've had years of practice when it comes to ignoring all things Sienna. Just another art form I've mastered over the years. Instead, I choose to focus all my attention on Mila. Her answer is the only thing which matters right now, and I can always deal with Sienna at a later date.

'What do you say? You coming to the game with me, princess?'

Both me and Sienna watch as her brows furrow in confusion. 'Me? 'She laughs, her eyes growing wide as she realizes this isn't a joke. 'Don't tell me you were being serious?'

'Deadly.' I growl out, unable to hold back. The suspense is killing me. I've never asked a chick to come to a game with me before but I know hands down if I'd asked anyone else, they would have jumped at the chance. What the hell is wrong with her? What's taking her so fucking long to decide. I don't do well with games unless I'm the one playing them. A little fact Mila is about to learn if she doesn't hurry up and answer me.

I can tell that Mila is trying to downplay her reaction, acting like it makes no difference to her whether she comes along as my plus one or not, but I can tell she's feeling the heat of the immense pressure which I've placed on her small, delicate shoulders. 'I already told you; hockey isn't my thing.'

I chose this moment, while her eyes are wide and her mouth is slightly open, to lean down and bring my face super close to her ear and whisper, 'no, but we both know what you like to do to me. I'm you're thing Mila, and don't think I'll ever let you forget it.'

Her breathing is unsteady as it catches in her throat and I watch, a sense of victory coursing through my veins as she swallows down hard. Mila might like to play hard to get but I know she wants me. She's desperate for me. I can see the heat of her insatiable hunger every time I look into her eyes. She's not doing herself any favors by resisting me. One way or another I will make her succumb to my needs. I've already told her as much. Mila Daniels is mine and she will never belong to another... not while there is still air in my lungs.

When I pull back, she looks at me and says, 'fine I'll come to your stupid game so long as you leave me alone.'

'Princess...'

'And Sienna comes with me too. Those are my terms.' She warns and I don't doubt she's being serious. 'Take it or leave it. The choice is yours.'

'Hey...' Sienna calls out from behind us. 'Don't drag me into your mess. This girl already has plans so you're gonna have to go and find someone else to play third wheel.'

'So cancel.' I bark back. It's not a request... it's a fucking demand. Sienna should know better than anyone to deny me what I want. Make no mistake, Sienna will be coming to the game and she'll be bringing Mila too.

CHAPTER TWENTY-TWO
JETT

I feel the heat of Sienna's eyes burning into the back of me the moment Mila heads out of the room.

Clenching my jaw and flaring my nostrils, I wait for her inevitable assault. Sienna hates to be kept in the dark, even when the details don't even concern her. She's not bothered so long as she's kept in the loop on everything which is around her.

'So... you wanna tell me what that was about?' Her voice is firm but also curious too. Sienna has known me longer than anyone else and she notices when I act out character, and this is one of those rare times. Just my look she had to be here to fucking witness it because now I won't hear the end of it.

At least she waited until Mila was out of ear shot. Sienna's beady little eyes never miss a damn thing and I'd be lying if I said it wasn't annoying as fuck sometimes. Just another valid reason why I don't want her living with me. I don't want Sienna at Greenmount, period... but there's jack shit I can do about it now.

'Well?' She presses, more instantly this time when I refuse to give her an answer. I don't need to answer to anyone, least of all my nosey ass little sister. I lean over the table and grab my sports bag, eager to get out of here before this conversation turns messy. 'Jett, you cannot leave me hanging like this. Spill it now.'

'I don't understand why you're getting so worked up about this. There's nothing to tell.' I lie effortlessly and I know she isn't about to buy my bullshit. She's like a fucking dog with a fucking toy. She'll keep going and going, refusing to let go until I have no choice but to let her into my sick and twisted mind.

'Don't even try to lie to me. I see the way you look at her...'

'Oh yeah? Maybe it's time you went to get your eyes tested because you can't see shit.' This whole conversation instantly gets my back up. Sure, Mila does things to me that no one else has even been able to do before, but that doesn't have to mean anything.

Does it?

My head is all over the place, Mila has knocked my guard down and everything else has fallen out of sync. That's all this is and soon enough everything will fall back into place and right itself. I just need to wait it out and get Sienna off my back in the process because she's a headache I really don't want or need.

My stubborn ass little sister pushes herself up from the table and walks over to me, trying her best to stand tall while squaring her small shoulders, foolishly thinking she'll be able to take me on. She might think she looks intimidating now, but the truth is Sienna couldn't intimidate a fly. 'Look, Jett... what and who you do is your business...'

'Damn fucking straight it is.' I cut her off, already knowing where this conversation is heading, but as usual

Sienna being a stubborn bitch and a real pain in my ass refuses to back the fuck down.

'I'm not discussing this with you, Cee...'

'Quit being a dick. Fuck whoever the hell you want around campus, I really couldn't care less but I'm telling you know, I draw the line when it comes to my friends. Leave Mila out of your bullshit, Jett. She doesn't need your drama.'

I snap my head back to look at her, my attention piqued. 'Why, what does she mean to you?' I question. Sienna has never been the person to care about anyone else but herself. That's where our similarities begin and end.

'Mila is my friend.' She exclaims and for the first time in her life she sounds genuine. 'I don't want to see her get hurt. Is that so bad? Is that so hard to believe?' She narrows her blue eyes at me and I know she means well; I just can't find it within myself to believe she truly means it.

Sienna has screwed her own fair share of people over during many years gone by. 'Plus, she deserves so much better than to be fucked around by you. Sure, you might have fallen in deep today, but what about tomorrow or the next day when you find someone else who appeals to you more?'

'Ouch.' I place my hand over my heart pretending that her empty words have hurt me. 'Careful, Cee... you might go and say something you won't be able to take back.'

'Whatever. I'm just trying to look out for a friend, is all.'

I shake my head, a ripple of disbelief flooding through me like a tsunami. 'I can see this for it truly is, so quit messing around. Quit trying to make this about Mila. I already told you; green isn't your color.'

'You think I'm jealous, don't you?'

'Aren't you?' It's a dickish move for sure, but I can't stop myself. Sienna has my back up and I'm instantly on the defensive, and I don't know what else to do. I don't know how to handle this kind of situation because I've never found myself in it before. I hate that Sienna can see straight through me. It unnerves me no fucking end.

'You wish.' She hurls back, her lips curling in disgust. 'Trust me, I wouldn't touch you if you were the last guy on earth. God knows what someone could catch from you.'

'Yeah, sure you wouldn't. We both know you'd jump on me if you had half the chance but that will never happen. I know that's what this is about. You can't have me so you don't want anyone to have me either, but I have news for you. Life doesn't work that way, Cee. We're family. Me and you could never happen… and Mila, she's a big girl and she can make her own decisions.'

I tried so hard not to bring up what almost happened between us because I know Sienna is easily embarrassed and humiliated by my rejection, but what else am I supposed to do when she's backing me into a corner? It's the only thing I can do which will make her back down. She's a feisty one and she's quick to get way above her station and sometimes as her older brother, it's my job to reign her back in before she goes too far.

I can tell Sienna is pissed at me. She's pissed at my behavior and attitude and I know I need to turn this around and fast. I need a favor and I need Sienna on my side for it to even become a possibility. I step closer and flash her my killer smile, signaling there's no hard feelings between us. 'Are you coming to the game tonight, or what?'

'That all depends…'

'On what?'

'On whether you're gonna quit your bitching if I say yes?'

'Deal.'

She smiles back at me and says, 'fine, but I'm not doing this for you. I'll be there to keep a close eye on Mila and also because I wouldn't miss the opportunity to watch you fall flat on your face.'

'Yeah, okay... we both know that isn't going to happen.' I reply confidently. 'But just do me a favor...'

'Another one?' She quips but she struggles to hide the smile on her face.

'When you see Mila, tell her to wear this for the game. It's important she wears it.' I toss the bundled-up fabric in her direction and she catches it, her reflexes on point as usual.

'Your jersey? Why do you want her to wear this? She told you she isn't into the game.' No, but she's into me, but I choose to keep that little fact to myself for now. Deep down Sienna knows the real reason why I want Mila to wear it. She doesn't voice it out loud but instead she looks at me and whistles as soon as she's arrived at her own conclusion. 'Shit... you've got it bad. You've got it a whole lot worse than I initially feared.'

'Are you kidding me?' I try to downplay her accusation, but fuck if I'm failing miserably. I'm not used to these kinds of situations. Usually, I'm the one who makes the rules. I'm the one who decides what happens, but not this time. I'm way out of my depth here and it's starting to show.

'Well why else would you ask her to wear your number? You and I both know that this will be the mother of all statements... but to who?' She presses.

'Exactly, but it's not for the reasons you're thinking. Today is a big game for me and I have a point to make. One that no one is going to miss if I do things this way, so do me a favor and do as I ask, okay?'

'Okay... fine. I guess this is one sure way to keep those desperate puck bunnies away from your bed. I fear many hearts will break today when they learn that the elusive Jett Jameson is no longer on the market. The new girl has gone and done the unthinkable and tamed the wicked beast.'

She's not fucking wrong, but I'm not foolish enough to admit it out loud. Instead, I reward her with a wicked smile as I turn to walk out of the door. Yes, Mila wearing my jersey will for sure keep the girls away while I focus all my attention on other pressing matters. More importantly it will prove more to that jock Cole Williams when he sees his ex, not only at my game but wearing my number... rooting me on from the stands.

I've never liked Cole and he's had this coming to him for an age. Now, finally after years of waiting, it's time for me to make that low life scum pay. Rivals for life, now on and off the ice. I look back at Sienna. 'I'll see you at the game. Don't be late. I need you, and this doesn't work if you don't follow the plan.'

She smiles back at me and shakes her head before shooing me off with a wave of her hand. 'Whatever. Get out of here, Loverboy.'

CHAPTER TWENTY-THREE
JETT

The cool air hits me as soon I step outside, and I take a moment to breathe it in.

It burns my lungs, reminding me how good it feels to be alive right in this moment. Today is going to be a good fucking day. I can already feel the thrill of victory deep in my bones, and it's a feeling I'm used to. A beautiful feeling which never gets old.

The reigning champions are back on the ice for the first time this season and there's not a single reason why we won't smash it... as fucking usual. Winning goes hand in hand with being a Giant. It comes naturally to us. Jett Jameson is the king of winning... on and off the ice and I smile freely at the thought.

'Hey...'

I open the door to my black jeep commander and look up at the voice calling out from the bottom of the driveway. A curvy blonde chick graces my vision and she's smiling brightly at me, but I don't really pay her much attention.

She obviously knows who I am and feels a little starstruck, but I don't recall her. I don't have too much time to think on it as I have places to go and a game to fucking win. I don't have time for anything else right now, especially what I'm guessing is one of Sienna's air-head friends.

'Jett,' she calls out as she comes closer, and I realize I'm not going to get out of here as fast as I thought.

'You looking for Sienna?' I ask, eager to get out of here and to where I need to be. Her face darkens and a flash of fury dances in her eyes. Weird, but hey-ho. This chick isn't my problem.

'Sienna?' She sounds hella confused. 'Who's Sienna?'

'Erm...' I'm at a loss at what to say to her and I really don't have time for delays. 'Maybe you're looking for Mila then? She's not here but you'll be able to catch her at the game later.' See, who says I can't be helpful.

She's silent for a moment before she nods back at me, signaling that she understands, her hands clasped in front of her, and she's showing no signs of moving out of my way.

'Cool...' I add, nodding to my car, signaling that she needs to move so I can back out of the drive. 'I'll see you there.'

'Actually...' she steps closer to me and a sudden sense of nervousness oozes out of her every pore. 'I'm not here to see them. I'm here to see you.'

Now she has my attention.

'Look, there's a game I have to get to. If you want a photo or an autograph, catch up with me after the game and we'll make it happen.' She probably thinks this is an open invitation to jump on my dick as soon as the game is over, but she'll be in for a shock when she finds Mila standing in the stands, wearing my number. Hell, the whole of Greenmount will be in for a shock and I'm so here for it.

It's not unusual for puck bunnies to grow mahoosive balls and come directly to my door, but this is early even by their standards. They usually hang out in the arena or in the bar afterward, doing everything they can to capture my attention. But mid-morning is new. Maybe they're trying to up their game this year. I hate to be the bearer of bad news, but that isn't going to be happening. I'm fairly confident no one will willingly approach me after today.

'I'm not here about the game.' She whispers. 'Don't you remember me?' Emotion seeps into her voice and when I look at her, her eyes swim with unshed tears... as though me not remembering who she is has actually hurt her somehow. I focus my eyes and look at her, really look at her hoping something might click in my mind, but nada. Try as I might, I can't place her. She doesn't even look familiar.

'Should I?' I ask, keeping my voice as calm as possible. The last thing I need is for her to have some kind of epic meltdown on my driveway. She doesn't say anything, and I really need to leave. 'Look, I hate to be rude, but I have somewhere to be like ten minutes ago. Game day, you know.' I take one last look at her before jumping in my car and rolling the engine.

What the fuck?

This bitch must be some kind of next level psycho and no way am I standing here dealing with that kind of bullshit. Not today of all days. If she turns up again then I'll have no choice but to deal with her, but for now all I can focus on is the game.

Fucking puck bunnies. Hopefully she will be the last of them turning up at my door. If they come here, then it's because I've decided to bring them back with me... not the other way round.

CHAPTER TWENTY-FOUR
MILA

'Remind me why I've agreed to this.'

I walk side by side with Sienna as we make our way to the arena and I feel well and truly out of my comfort zone. Campus is completely packed out and the game doesn't even start for ages yet. I swear if ever there was a time to feel claustrophobic then the time would be now.

'You agreed to this because you're a nice person and you didn't want me to endure the endless torture all by myself.' Sienna beams back at me.

'I'm pretty sure the deal was that I'd only come if you agreed to come with me. Not the other way around.'

'Same thing.' She laughs and it's contagious. Even though my anxiety is through the roof right now, I can't help but laugh a little too.

I move to the side to allow a herd of giggling girls to hurry past us, and I wish I shared their enthusiasm. 'Sienna, can I ask you a serious question?'

'That all depends on whether you want a serious answer or not.'

I think on this for a moment. Sienna has always struck me as being the kind of person who will tell you what's on her mind, without even thinking twice about it. I think that's why I liked her initially, and now when she's the only person who can give me a little insight into Jett, I'm not sure I'll be able to handle the truth. But what choice do I have, really? I need to know what I'm getting myself involved with here and Sienna is the only person who can help me.

'Why do you always do what Jett tells you if you don't like him?' It sounds innocent enough, and the smirk on her lips lets me know she already knew this would be about Jett. She stops walking and turns her head toward me so she can get a better read on me. 'I should have known this would have been about him, but what makes you think I don't like him?'

'Seriously? You really want me to answer that?' I wait for her response, but she just raises her eyebrow at me, encouraging me to continue. 'You can feel the tension simmering between the two of you from miles away.' I confess, and a small part of me wonders if I've overstepped the mark.

I don't know what I expected from her, but after a moment she slides her arm into mine and pulls me close. 'Just because I think he's a dick, that doesn't mean I don't like him. Sure, he's a pain in the ass at the best of times, but that's just his way. I'll let you into a secret... hidden beneath his fake bad boy bravado lies a heart of gold. He's a good guy really, he just doesn't want anyone figuring it out.'

We walk through the large iron gates and walk towards the stands, and the atmosphere instantly changes once we're inside the arena. 'Can I ask what happened between the two of you?'

'Worried you've got competition?' She quizzes and I feel the heat of my embarrassment rush to my cheeks and I know it has nothing to do with the sharp drop in temperature.

'Er... should I be?' I feel my face scrunch in confusion. I know I shouldn't have gone there with Jett, that much is already a given. But the last thing I want to do is to step on anyone's toes and make heaps of awkward situations for myself. Especially if I have to live with these two.

'I'd love to tell you, Mila, but a lady never tells.' A small ghost of a smile plays on her lips and I don't know if she's enjoying my discomfort or if she's playing with me. I'm starting to regret ever opening my mouth.

'I shouldn't have asked.' I mouth quietly. 'Tell me to mind my own business, but I was curious is all. After all, we have to live together and it kind of felt something must have happened between the two of you judging by how closed off and standoffish you both are when you're together.'

At my confession, Sienna is quick to throw her head back before letting out a mighty roar of laughter. 'Wait... let me get this straight. You thought me and Jett used to be a thing?'

I narrow my eyes, trying to understand how I could have gotten this all kinds of wrong. 'Weren't you?' Now I'm the one who's confused. If they weren't together and didn't have some kind of messy break-up, then why do they seem to hate each other so much?

'Fuck no.' She shakes her head and her eyes are glistening with tears of laughter. 'Shit, I have to give it to you, Mila. Your imagination is pretty wild.' She waggles her eyebrows at me like she's in on some top secret I don't know about. 'I like you, so I'm about to tell you something, but I don't want this going around campus...'

'Shoot.' I reply with zero hesitation, desperate to hear everything and anything she can tell me about Jett. 'You have my word that no one will ever hear it from me.'

'Okay... I'll trust you. You didn't hear this from me, okay?' I nod in agreement, so vigorously that I'm surprised my head doesn't fall off. 'Jett doesn't hate me. He just hates having me around because I'm too much of a close connection to him. Now that I'm here he can no longer live his life the way he's used to. He has to be more discreet...'

'I'm so not following where this is going.' I admit on a whisper.

'Okay, let me put it this way. If you were used to calling the shots around here, doing whatever the hell you wanted with zero questions asked, how would you feel if your little sister turned up and could watch your every move?'

It takes me a hot minute to process her words and realize what she's saying but as soon as they register in my mind my mouth falls open and almost hits the floor. 'You're Jett's sister?' The shock and relief in my voice is evident and I know Sienna doesn't miss it.

'You heard it here first. I'm Jett's biggest secret, so please make sure you don't let it slip. If you do, then I can promise it won't end well for either of us. The last thing Jett wants or needs is anyone finding out I'm related to him.'

'Wow...' I allow the words to hang in the air between us for a few seconds. 'I really thought you were bitter ex's or something. I would have never guessed the two of you were related—at all.'

'Yeah well, I guess the world works in mysterious ways.' She leans forward and grabs her drink before looking me square in the eye. 'I know Jett better than anyone else... probably better than he knows himself. Do me a favor and be careful when you're around him. Jett isn't the best when it comes to treating girls the way they should be. He has quite the reputation around here and don't take this the wrong way, but you strike me as the type of girl who wears her heart on her sleeve.'

Sienna looks straight at me and her eyes are full of genuine concern. My heart stammers in my chest as she confirms what I already know. Jett Jameson is dangerous. He's a monster and I should be doing everything I can to stay away from him. But when I'm with him he makes me feel like I've never felt before.

Jett makes me feel validated. He makes me feel wanted and most important, he makes me feel alive; a feeling I lost many years ago when my mom suddenly became dependent on me.

Jett takes away my pain. He manages to break into my mind and remove all of my traumas without him even realizing they're a part of me. I remember my mom always telling me when I was younger that if something was too good to be true then it probably was and to run away at the first opportunity.

But how can I run away from someone who I'm going to be living with for the next nine months, if not longer? I'm not strong enough to hold him off. The magnetic connection between us is far too strong, and now that I know he exists, now that I've had a taste of what he has to offer, there's no way I'm going to be able to walk away from him. There's no way I'll be able to forget her ever existed.

'I like you, Mila, I really do, and I'd hate for my heartless brother to eat you alive. If you allow him to get too close, one day soon he'll break that sweet little heart of yours and there's no way you'll be able to put it back together again.'

I smile, trying to brush away her concern but on the other hand I already know what she's telling me is true. 'I don't think you need to worry about any of that happening.'

'Ah, but I do. I see the way you look at him and I know this can only end one way—in disaster. I'm not saying don't go and have some fun with him, that's up to you... I'm just telling you to be careful in the process.'

We take our seats in silence as I think on what Sienna has Just divulged to me. I keep telling myself I don't need to worry about Jett because nothing serious is ever going to happen between us anyway.

We made a mistake.

A mistake neither one of us wants to repeat again. I was in the wrong place at the wrong time and now I'm the one who's foolishly agreed to play along with his stupid game so he doesn't have to deal with heaps of girls at his feet. Personally, I can't figure out his logic. I don't see how me pretending to be his girlfriend is going to change that fact. But for now, I'm happy to humor him—so long as it gets him off my back.

'Oh, before I forget... Jett asked me to give you this.'

'What is it?' I ask, suspicion heavy in my tone as she reaches into her bag and pulls out a familiar looking blue piece of fabric.

'His Jersey. He told me to tell you to wear it for the game.'

I shake my head. No way am I sitting in this arena wearing his jersey. Does this guy want me to help him, or is this some kind of sick and twisted set up so I get attacked by the crazy psycho girls who follow his every move? 'I'm not wearing it.' I try to hand the jersey back to Sienna. A flash of shock creeps onto her face, but it's gone just as fast as it arrived.

'Why not?'

'Have you seen the number of girls who are here. Standing in the arena, cheering your brother on, just hoping to score with him? Have you heard them all chanting his name? No way am I putting that on and willingly making myself a target.'

'I don't think that's why he asked you to wear it.'

'Maybe... maybe not, but it's not a risk I'm willing to take.' My voice is firm and final, but just like her brother, Sienna isn't about to back down.

'Mila... Jett isn't open to his emotions. He's more closed off than Fort Knox. He doesn't know how to express himself, but I can tell he likes you. Like I said, he's a guy with a big heart but he's also got a big ego to match. If Jett has asked you to wear it, then it obviously means something significant to him.'

I know what Sienna is trying to do. This whole act has Jett written all over it. He's obviously found the time to back his little sister into a corner, expecting her to do his dirty work, but I'm not about to fall into his trap.

Not now... not ever.

I quickly excuse myself, telling Sienna I need to use the little girls room, but the truth is, I need to take a moment to process my thoughts. I need some time to think and clear my head.

I leave the stands and go down the hall, and everywhere I turn, girls are everywhere. I've never witnessed so many in one place. And Jett obviously wants to feed me to the wolves. I should have stayed where, was because the moment I step through the rest room door, Jett is not on my heels. I see his angry face glaring back at me through the mirror. His eyes are wild and his nostrils flare when he takes me in—a sure sign if ever there was one that I've majorly pissed him off.

I've done what he asked. I'm here like I said I would be, but I draw the line when it comes to putting myself in danger.

Before I have a chance to turn around or say a single word, a moment to fight my case, Jett quickly closes the distance between us. The overwhelming scent of him instantly disarms me, leaving me weak and vulnerable. My composure quickly drops to non-existent by the time he's pressed his muscular body flush against mine.

'You wouldn't be in here hiding, would you princess?' The accusation rolls heavily from his tongue, but I can't speak. My voice has lost all basic functionality and all I can manage is a quick shake of my head. 'Good girl. Now turn around so I can get a better look at you.' He demands, his voice husky and deadly.

He doesn't need to ask me twice. My body responds to him like my lungs respond to air. I can try to deny it all I like, but the truth is I'm desperate for him. Hell, if this is how my mom feels when it comes to alcohol then I can totally empathize with her addiction. He's impossible to stay away from. Always simmering in your mind, promising you'll stop after you've had one last final taste.

Trying to convince yourself you can move on when you've had one more hit. Rinse and repeat.

Jett Jameson is quickly becoming my very own personal form of crack and the more time I spend with him, the more I'm convinced that there's no way I'll ever be able to walk away from him.

Jett Jameson will be my downfall, and there's not a god damn thing I can do about it.

His jade green eyes continue to search mine, and I feel completely exposed, like he can see deep down into my soul. He opens me up like no one else and a small part of me wants to expose my soul to him—giving him everything I have to offer, but it would never be enough.

'Strip.' is all he says on a heated whisper.

'Excuse me...' I stammer, suddenly finding my voice again.

'You heard me, princess. I said strip.' A dose of danger dances in his eyes and his jaw sets, holding himself firm and strong.

'Are you insane? We're in the middle of a public restroom.' I exclaim, trying to snap him back to reality and make him see sense, that his demands are hideous.

'And? No one can see you.' He snickers. 'My whole body covers you. You're safe with me princess.' Amusement creeps into his tone when he says the last words and I could laugh too. We both know that I'm anything but safe when I'm alone with him.

'Why is this so important to you?' I question, struggling to understand why he's still pressing the issue. Isn't having me here good enough? 'You asked me to come, and here I am.' He also asked me to be his fake girlfriend, which I'm still thinking about, but from the way Jett is acting, I'm starting to wonder if he's already convinced himself that it's a done deal.

I can understand his first two requests, but I'm struggling to understand what's so important about wearing his Jersey and why he's so keen to keep pushing it.

'I already told you,' He licks his bottom lip as his eyes roam my face and my whole body turns to liquid butter. I need to be so much stronger than this. I need to get my head together if I'm going to survive the next nine months of my life while I'm living with him. 'It's a sure-fire way to keep the heat off me and more importantly, my dick... unless you don't mind sharing.'

I open my mouth to argue with him but quickly close it again. I take a few moments to compose myself before speaking again and when I do, I hold my voice calm and steady. 'And I already told you, I'm nothing like the usual girls you manage to trick into your bed.

'Trick?' He raises a questioning brow and I instantly regret my wording. 'From memory I didn't trick you into my bed, princess. No, from what I remember you came willingly and, in more ways, than one.'

I laugh in his face. 'Yeah... I bet that's what you say to all the girls.' I try to keep my voice even and steady, but it falls from my lips on a breathless whisper.

'Would it surprise you if I told you I've never once said that to another girl?' He breathes, and the heat of his minty breath intoxicates me some more. 'You're the first girl I've ever allowed to stay the night in my room. You're the first girl I've ever thought about wearing my jersey, let alone asking you. Princess. I never thought I'd admit this, but you do things to me I never thought possible. I can't get the thought of you out of my head and it's driving me insane. You've got me in a motherfucking chokehold and I am so here for it.'

My eyes search his and all I can see is a deep sense of hunger in his predatorial gaze. Is he telling me the truth or playing games with me? It's really hard to tell because his beautiful angular face is always set, serious and deadly. My mind is on overdrive as I try to process his words, desperate to find some kind of smart ass reply but once again Jett Jameson has rendered me speechless. He has me in a chokehold too and he sure as hell knows it.

He uses this moment, a moment when my guard is well and truly down, to make his move. His warm minty breath invades my senses, totally disarming me and I succumb to all things Jett. 'Please...' he whispers against my neck, causing all the small hairs to stand tall. 'Do this one thing for me. I promise you won't regret it.'

Jett offering me a promise should set off all kinds of alarm bells ringing, but I'm in too deep now to even think about the warning signs. 'What's in it for me?' I question, my head in a cloudy haze.

He doesn't falter as he presses his warm lips to mine, his whole-body flush against me and I gasp when I feel the heat of his solid erection press against my stomach. 'You'll see... all I ask is that you have a little faith.' Is all he says before he pulls away, leaving my body cold, empty and void of his touch. A touch I'm fast becoming too dependent on.

Jett flashes me a quick panty dropping smile before he turns and leaves the restroom, and then he's gone—all before I have a chance to pick my jaw up from the floor.

CHAPTER TWENTY-FIVE
JETT

I skate out onto the ice, gliding like a pro as I take in a deep lungful of air, and I know that I'm home.

The crowd goes wild, screaming out my name and a rush of adrenaline courses through my veins. This right here... the ice, the game, the freedom... this is the reason I wake up and get out of bed every single morning. This game is what forces me to keep pushing myself to be bigger... to be better.

'You ready?' Bennett shouts across to me and I nod back knowingly. I know what's expected of me and there hasn't been a single game where I haven't delivered.

I look out toward the stands while warming up, Imagine Dragons booming out of the speakers around us, and my chest tightens. A sharp unexpected stab of pride shoots through me, like an icy arrow straight through my damaged heart when I take in the sight of Mila. She looks so small from where I'm standing, but so important. Mila Daniels looks like the star of the fucking show as she shows her support for the Giants and for me in the best way possible. Support by wearing my jersey. My fucking number, for all to see.

Even the Royal Ravens.

Cole is going to lose his shit when he comes out and witnesses his ex in my jersey... displaying her loyalty, claiming herself as mine for the whole arena to see and I am so fucking here for it.

To be honest, I'm shocked more than anything. I never thought Mila would go for it. She's sure made a habit of going against me and doing the total opposite of what I'm used to when it comes to standard behavior of girls. She's something else for sure, but I'm feeling good that she's finally listened to me and has actually done something I've asked her to do.

Maybe I should have warned her about the downside of wearing my jersey. After all she's standing in the middle of an arena wearing my number with a bunch of desperate puck bunnies surrounding her. Some I've fucked, and the rest are desperate to get on my hit, or should I say dick, list. She's getting death glares left right and center. I can feel the anger radiating off every single one of them. Either Mila hasn't noticed it, or she's majorly good at turning a blind eye.

I don't need to be too worried though. If I've learned anything in the short time I've had the pleasure of knowing Mila, it's that she can for sure handle her own. Plus, even though we don't see eye to eye most times, I know Sienna will have her back. Mila is a tough cookie. She'll be able to handle it... but I'm quick to remind myself it's not just the puck bunnies I want to make a bold statement to.

No... the main person this little set up is for is none other than Cole Williams. It's high time that motherfucker was knocked back down the food chain. I don't know what it is with him but he seriously thinks he's something that he's not. Something he can never be... and that something is me.

He's way above his station. I've been eager to find a way to damage him and I couldn't believe my luck when he turned up at my door, pleading his case to Mila, begging for her to take his sorry ass back. It was like the universe had finally heard me... actually listened to my prayers and decided to answer them.

Now it's time to watch this shit show unfold, and I am so fucking here for it. All... day... and all night long.

I laugh when *whatever it takes* booms out of the speakers... signaling my time to leave and get ready for the first game of the season and the irony isn't lost on me.

CHAPTER TWENTY-SIX
MILA

'Fuck.'

'What's wrong?' Sienna asks as she takes a seat beside me, laden with drinks and snacks for the game. I'm glad to see someone is prepared and ready to settle down for the game. Me on the other hand, I want to stand up and make a run for it. How could I have been so fucking stupid?

'Did you know who the Giants were playing?' I ask as she hands me a soda, her face calm and neutral.

'No. Do I look like someone who pays attention to all of this crap? I'm here for you, remember. That was the deal, no?'

My eyes grow wide as I look at Sienna, hoping she can see the panic bubbling deep inside me. 'I can't be here.' I whisper, so quiet that I doubt she even hears me.

'Why, what's happened?' I look of concern creeps onto her face. 'I thought you and Jett were good now.' She flashes her eyes to his shirt, and I roll my eyes. This is so much bigger than Jett's fucking shirt. This is so much bigger than I could have ever imagined.

'I didn't know they were playing the Raven's.'

'Neither did I. All I know is this is a pretty big game. I think the Ravens are the Giant's biggest rivals.' She takes a sip off her soda before adding. 'Yeah, I'm sure I've heard Jett bitching about them before. I don't usually pay much attention to him, but I remember the Raven's because they're from Ravendale, right?'

'Right.' I try to shrink back into my seat, but it's no good. We're right at the front. Behind the glass. No doubt this is Jett's doing to make sure we have the best seats in the house.

'What's the big deal anyway? I thought hockey wasn't your thing?' Her eyebrows waggle back at me, and I can tell she's finding some kind of amusement in my discomfort. Sienna is supposed to be my friend. She's supposed to be on my side.

I lean forward hoping to hide myself behind her but it's no good. I feel completely exposed. Call me paranoid but I can feel hundreds of curious eyes burning into me. I've never been a big fan when it comes to attention. That's Skye's role in our friendship. She's always been the one front and center, more than happy to bask in the limelight, and I've always been happy to hide in the background, basking in her shadow. But Skye isn't here to save me now. 'Hockey isn't my thing, and for good reason...'

'You've lost me, kid.' Sienna's brows furrow together as confusion sweeps across her face.

'My ex... he's a Raven. He's their goalie and he's gonna lose his shit if he sees me here.' Doesn't Sienna understand what kind of position Jett has put me in? Yes, me and Cole are history and I'd love to hurt him, but I can think of better ways to do the job instead of putting myself straight into the middle of World War three. Is this why Jett was so insistent for me to wear his number?

Jett gave me a load of bullshit which I foolishly fell for. He had me convinced by me wearing his number was so I could help him out, make a statement to the girls on campus that he was done with his fuck boy ways. A way to keep them from hounding him all the time, but now I'm convinced that wasn't the only reason Jett was so insistent about it. No, the more I think about it, the more I'm convinced he's asked me to wear this so that he can make a bold ass statement to Cole.

Not content with beating him on the ice, he's now wanting to make the stakes personal and he's claiming me as his own so he can class this as another win against Cole.

It takes a minute but I watch as the realization creeps in and glistens in Sienna's eyes. 'Shit, girl. I guess it sucks to be you right now.'

'This isn't funny.' I bite back when a small smirk creeps onto her lips.

'Not for you no… but Jett is one sick and twisted son of a bitch.'

'I'm not following.' Does Sienna know something that I don't? My heart pounds deep in my chest, and I know I'm right. I know he's selfishly used me for his own sick and twisted games. Everything he's said to me, all the bullshit he gave me back in the restroom wasn't real. He was playing with me and he played me good. And I'm the fool who recklessly fell for it, allowing him to convince me he actually liked me when all I really was, was nothing more than a means to an end. I hate myself for being so gullible and so stupid.

'Jett's a smart son of a bitch. Sick and twisted for sure, but he sure knows what he's doing.' She shakes her head like she can't believe she fell for his bullshit too. 'There's me thinking he'd gone and caught feelings for you. I mean, he seriously had me convinced, but he obviously played us both and instead decided to use you as part of his plan.'

'Plan?' I exclaim, disbelief flooding my voice. 'What plan?' I swallow down on the lump of emotion forming at the back of my throat, and my eyes glisten with unshed tears as they threaten to spill over. It's no secret that I've been through some bullshit in my life but I don't think I've ever been humiliated like this, especially by some jerk of a guy who thinks he's better than God himself. My body trembles violently as a rush of anger courses through me and it takes everything I have to keep myself seated. I swear if I get hold of him, I'm going to make this son of a bitch pay.

'Oh boy... I knew he'd go and do something like this. I warned him to stay away from you. I knew he'd end up using you and hurting you in the process.' I flinch as her words hit me hard. If Sienna can see it then everyone else on campus is going to know I was taken for a fool by none other than Jett Jameson. I've only ever been just another number on his hit list, and I was too blind to see it. 'What better way to piss off the opposition by making his mark on the other players girl. Jett has always been a ruthless, selfish son of a bitch, but I have to admit, even this is a step too far for him.'

'I'm no one's girl.' I bite out through gritted teeth, desperately trying to keep my emotions in check. I'm in the middle of a packed-out arena, with ninety percent of *team Jameson* surrounding me. No way will I allow any one of them to witness me break down and cry. Not a single one.

'Sure, you're not...' Sienna nods empathetically, but there isn't much conviction in her voice. 'But take a look there, Mila...' she points to a screen and my eyes reluctantly follow. 'See that kiss cam... that kinda says different. You're in Jett's jersey. You're wearing his number for all to see. To Greenmount and beyond, you're his now. Wearing a players jersey has more meaning than an engagement ring around here.'

I want to leave, but I know if I do then I'll be allowing Jett to win, and one thing I have never been is a quitter. I'm not about to allow the likes of Jett Jameson and his vindictive ways to get the better of me. I've fought bigger battles and there's no way I'll stand back and allow him to defeat me.

Against my better judgement I remain seated, thunder thrumming in my veins as I watch the idolized guys coming out of the tunnel, Imagine Dragons roaring in our ears as hundreds of girls jump up and down screaming Jett's name. He could have picked any girl in this arena to wear his jersey, but he didn't. He picked me, and not because he liked what he saw. No, this sick and twisted jerk did it so he could win some stupid turf war with my ex-boyfriend.

I don't know how, but by some miracle I managed to survive.

I endured the whole game without any physical damage. It's a shame I can't say the same thing for the damage which has been done to me on the inside.

Sienna has been true to her word and has stayed by my side like she promised and for that I'm grateful. Either she knows just how much of a jerk her brother is, or she actually pitied me. She refrained from mentioning Jett again. She cheered him on and got into the spirit of the game, but I just couldn't find it within myself to join her or match her energy.

'They won.' she exclaims down my ear as soon as the players retreat, excitement dancing in her eyes. 'But what I want to know is, have you been converted yet?'

Even though I'm burning with insatiable rage on the inside, I can't help but offer her a small smile. 'No. I told you; hockey really isn't my thing and I don't think I'll ever be converted.'

'Hmmm.' She muses, more to herself. 'I wonder if my asshat of a brother didn't choose to royally fuck up anything that's good for him if you'd be here feeling a whole lot different right now.'

I shake my head, still trying to keep a handle on my emotions. 'I guess we'll never know.' It's a bold statement but nothing but the truth. 'Look, I'd love to stay and hang out...' the sarcasm rolls freely from my tongue and I know Sienna doesn't miss it, 'but I need to get out of here.'

'Wow.' Her eyes widen in disbelief.

'What?'

'Never ever did I think you were the type of person to allow some guy to run you out of town.'

I laugh and for the first time since I figured out Jett's evil master plan, it's actually genuine. 'I'm not letting anyone run me out of town.' When she narrows her eyes, I can tell she isn't buying it. I hold my hands up, trying to protest my innocence as I say, 'honestly. I have work.'

'You work too?'

'Sure I do. I decided to keep my old job back in Coldwater. Figured I could use the extra income while I'm studying.' That's not the only thing its good for. Thankfully I now have a valid excuse to get out of here and I don't have to pin the blame on Jett, even though he is the reason but I'm not going to admit out loud just how much his conniving plan has destroyed me. My mind has been screaming at me, warning me to steer clear of him ever since I laid my eyes on him, and did I listen? No, I didn't, and look where that's landed me.

Jett has made me look like a fool in front of the whole of Campus. He played me for the fool he knew I was.

'What should I tell Jett?' She enquires. 'He's going to be looking for you when he comes out.'

Yeah, I don't doubt it. He'll love nothing more than to flaunt me in front of Cole. This has never been about me. This has always been about point scoring. Finding a way to get one over on Cole. Jett must have thought he'd hit the jackpot when he turned up at our apartment and figured out the connection. 'Tell him what you want. I really don't care.' I quickly shuffle out of his jersey, scrunching it into a ball before shoving it into her unsuspecting hands. 'Make sure you give him this too because I have no need for it anymore.'

'Shit... he's really fucked up this time.'

I offer another smile in her direction and stand, slowly edging past her. 'Yep, but he isn't my problem anymore.'

CHAPTER TWENTY-SEVEN
JETT

The euphoria seeps through my veins, the electricity thrumming through my body like wildfire. Another glorious victory to add to the never-ending list and it sure feels good.

It's feels so fucking good.

'I bet you enjoyed that, didn't you?' A familiar voice calls out behind me as I make it into the tunnel, the rest of my team celebrating before me. My body is ablaze with adrenaline from the win and I don't think twice when I turn around and come face to face with Cole.

'More than you could ever imagine.' My chest instinctively puffs out, my inner alpha taking over as he slowly moves towards me, and I can tell he's pissed. His black hair is ruffled, stuck to the side of his face with sweat and his nostrils are flare as he tries to regulate his breathing. Anyone looking at him right now wouldn't think anything was off. They'd think it was just his body coming down, trying to rest after a vigorous workout, but I know different.

Cole is raging on the inside.

Absolutely fuming that I've made a fool of him on the ice and also made an example of him in front of his whole team and minimal fans. Nothing is safe when I'm about. A hockey game or the girl you've been fucking. I know he saw Mila wearing my jersey. It would have riled him no end that his girl, or his ex-girl has moved sides and was wearing their rival's number.

When Mila finds out what I've done, she isn't going to be happy, but I'm sure I'll be able to work my charms on her and convince her it was just a game tactic, but also for the greater good.

'You might have won this time...' Cole comes closer to me, his shoulders squaring like he's gearing himself up for a fight. Now that is a sight I would pay to see. 'But this isn't over.'

'Oh yeah?' I laugh in his face. 'Say's who... you?'

Without so much as a second thought he throws his arm out and punches me in the shoulder, catching me off guard but I'm quick to bounce back. The pain radiates down my arm but fuck if I'm about to let it show.

'I'll let you have that one, dickface.' I move closer to him, my large frame towering over his as he glares back at me. 'Touch me again, and I'll do more than fuck you up on the ice. I've already fucked your ex, so how about I move onto your mom?'

He swings again but this time I'm faster. My reflexes on point as I grip his hand in my wrist. 'You won't get away with this, Jameson.'

'No?' I laugh in his face some more, before leaning over him and he cowers back against the wall. 'And how are you going to stop me?'

'I know what you've done. You can pretend you care about Mila all you damn well like but we both know you're only making a run for her because you think it's the quickest way you can get to me.'

'Looks like my plan worked then, didn't it?'

'She'll come around. She'll soon see you for the jerk you are.'

I smile at him, the conviction in his voice has me thinking he truly believes the bullshit which is coming out of his mouth. 'Until then, you can rest easy in the knowledge that it's my bed she climbs into every night, and my name which leaves her lips on a delicate moan.'

My words affect him more than I thought possible as he uses all he has to push me back, but I stand tall. 'This isn't over.' He shouts back at me as I turn to walk away knowing that my job here is done.

We've won the first game of the season which was a given. Mila has declared to the world that she's mine, and now all I have to do is head back to the apartment and enjoy the fruits of my Labor.

What's not to love about my fucking life... and not a desperate puck bunny in sight.

This is the life.

CHAPTER TWENTY-EIGHT
MILA

I couldn't get into my car and out of Greenmount fast enough.

Thankfully when I told Sienna I needed to get out of there so I could get to work on time, she didn't put up much of a fight.

The warm air hits me as I walk through the door to Frankie's and for the first time today, I finally feel a sense of calm wash over me. I knew I shouldn't have played into Jett's words. He's the biggest fuck boy in Greenmount. Obviously, he was only using me, trying to get close to me and whisper me endless sweet nothings so he could get something out of me.

I was nothing more than a measly pawn in his sick and twisted games, and now I'm the one who's going to have to pay the price.

Everyone on campus witness my stupid display of support. They'll all be gossiping about the two of us. How the new girl from Coldwater... the Raven's ex has managed to tame the villainous playboy. How am I supposed to go back there now and face the music. It's absolutely humiliating.

I know I'll have to go. I'll have to drive back to Greenmount as soon as my shift is over, because the only thing worse than facing Jett and his masses, is facing my mom and crawling back to that rundown apartment with my tail firmly between my legs. Not going to happen. I've worked too hard to get to where I am to give it all up because of some stupid and reckless mistake. There's no way I'm going to give up on my dreams just because I fell into bed with the devil.

'So...' Skye barrels over to the bar as soon as she sees me. 'How did it go?'

I look at her blankly, unsure what she's asking of me. 'How did what go?'

'The game...' she huffs as she pulls herself up to sit on the barstool. 'Don't tell me you didn't even go.'

'Yeah... it was okay, I guess.' I narrow my eyes at her. 'Why are you so interested.'

Her eyes widen as she looks at me in disbelief. 'Because my guy was playing and I want to know how he got on. Did they win? Please tell me they killed the Raven's. Please tell me that Cole was finally put in his rightful place... to the fucking Kirb.'

I let out a low whistle as I busy my hands by wiping the sides. This is not a conversation I want to be having with Skye right now. She doesn't even know about me and Jett, let alone how much he humiliated me today. I know I'll have to tell her at some point, and I'll have to do it fast before her new boyfriend spills all the beans. 'The Giants won but I wasn't really paying much attention. You know I can't lose myself in the game.'

'Maybe next time you could invite me to one and I'll show you how it's done, babe.' I don't doubt it.

'How about I invite you, instead.' A deep voice rumbles beside us I look up and see Bennett, Skye's new fuck piece watching us. His smile is huge, and you can tell the winning buzz is still coursing through his veins.

'Seriously?' Skye squeals with excitement and a wave of nausea overcomes me. She looks so happy, and I'm made up for her. But I can't shake the feeling that Bennett is up to no good. Sure, I have no reason not to trust him except he's best friends with the guy who's just happily fucked me over and ruined my life.

'Anything for you babe.' He grins back before leaning in for a kiss. When he's finally had his fill of my best friend, he eventually turns his attention to me. 'I saw you out in the stands.' A wicked smirk creeps onto his lips and I silently pray to all things holy that he'll drop it. I need him to kill this conversation before it's even started.

'Can I get you a drink?' I ask, trying my damned hardest to change the subject.

'Sure, I'll have an orange juice and whatever this little lady is having.' I go to turn away, ready to serve up their drinks, but as I suspected, Bennett hasn't finished. 'I also saw you repping Jett's shirt. I have to admit, I was shocked, man. No one has ever worn his shirt before. It's not really a Jett thing, but you seem to have rubbed him up the wrong way, for sure.' I feel the heat of my embarrassment rush to my cheeks as well as Skye's blue eyes blazing into mine. 'You've sure gotten under his skin like no one else. And those puck bunnies aren't going to be happy about it.'

'Whoa... back up a couple of steps...' Skye jumps in, her eyes wide like a deer caught in the headlights. 'What's he talking about, Mila?' She questions, backing me into a corner until I'm forced to answer her.

'I just wore a Giant jersey is all. It's no big deal.' The lack of conviction in my voice is evident and I'd love nothing more than for the ground to open up and swallow me whole. I've made such a mess of my life today, and now I can't go back and change any of it.

'Nah... you can't downplay this. She wore our Captain's jersey, after he requested it.'

'Demanded it more like.' I correct through gritted teeth.

'Ah, but was that before or after you shared his bed?' He waggles his eyebrows at me, and I hear Skye gasp. This cannot be happening. Obviously, Jett and all of his friends are grade A jerks who love embarrassing people. They clearly like to kick people when they're down, for sure.

'Mila... is this true?' Skye cuts in,' because if it is then I think you and me need to have a little talk.'

'There's nothing to say.' I narrow my eyes at Bennett in silent warning, hoping he interprets my meaning. *Thanks for dropping me in the shit.* 'I don't have anything to say to him or about him. He made his feelings clear when he used me to get back at Cole.' I know Bennett will be in the loop with Jett's devious plan, because he's obviously in on everything else.

'What does Cole have to do with any of this.'

I look at my best friend, 'Apparently Cole is Jett's biggest rival, so he decided to play me for a fool. He made a move on me so he could use me to prove a point to Cole. End of. He's done what he set out to do. It's done. Finished.'

'I wouldn't say that. Didn't you see what happened after the game?' Now Bennett has my attention.

'No. I had to leave to get ready for my shift.' I wait patiently for him to tell me what happened and my heart pounds in my chest, my anxiety suddenly on high alert again.

The look on his face tells me whatever happened when I'd upped and left isn't going to be good.

'Cole decided to play the big guy. He spat his dummy out because they lost the game and he tried to take his bullshit out on Jett, not happy that you could move on so easily, especially with someone who plays for the Giants.'

'Shit...' I had no idea. I know I shouldn't feel bad. Cole has everything that's coming to him, but I can't help but feel a little guilty when I'm unintentionally involved. 'But you know that's what Jett wanted, right? That's why he set me up.'

Bennett throws his head back on a roaring laugh and when he looks at me his face is humorous but also a little serious. 'Is that what you think? Cole and Jett have been gunning for each other for years. You didn't detonate the bomb, Mila... that was already ticking long before you came on to the scene.'

'I find that hard to believe. If Jett didn't want to use me to get back at Cole, then why give me his jersey so Cole could see. Jett knew that would have raised some kind of reaction out of him.'

'Sure, it would. He's a red-blooded male like all of us. He's territorial and so is Jett but I know that guy better than most and I've seen the way he's acted since you showed up at Greenmount. I don't know what you've done to him but trust me it's for the better. Sure, he might have used the whole jersey situation to antagonize Cole, but I know my guy and I know he'd never let anyone wear his number unless he had genuine feelings for them.'

I'm at a loss for words. I don't know what to believe anymore. 'Sienna even said it was all part of his plan. Why would she lie.'

Another laugh escapes him. 'Because that's what Sienna does. I get that you're new around Greenmount kid, but damn, you sure have a lot to learn. If you want my advice… ignore Sienna. Her word is usually worthless and heavily laced with poison. Once you've finished your shift, head back to Greenmount and have it out with Jett if it makes you feel any better, but mark my words, you've made a mark on him for sure. He's an ass, just don't give up on him. Not so soon, anyway.'

⁓⁓

My shift is over before I know it, and now it's time for me to face the music. I don't want to do this, but I know it's better to get it out of the way now and then it's over and done with. I have to live with Jett for the next nine months and the last thing I want is for any awkwardness to kick in between us.

I'll go back and I'll allow him to say his piece, if that's what he wants. If not, I'm more than happy to pretend none of this ever happened and move on with my life.

The cold air hits me when I step outside, the rain coming down hard and fast. Skye and Bennett are hot on my heels, and I know these two are going to become inseparable. I'd think it was cute if I wasn't so pissed off with my own personal life right now.

'Are you shittin' me?' I call out into the void when I come to a stop at my truck. Just when I thought today couldn't get any worse, the universe likes to hurl another spanner into the works. As if I haven't been tested enough.

'What's wrong?' Skye is at my side instantly.

'I've got a flat.' I don't even have a spare in the back as I used that a few months ago and never got around to getting a replacement. 'How am I supposed to drive back now? I have classes super early tomorrow too so it's not like I can crash at my moms and catch the bus.' I lean down and look at my tire, a large tear has been cut down the middle. 'This wasn't caused by a stray nail in the road. Look...' I exclaim. 'Someone has targeted my truck intentionally.'

'Do you think it was Cole?' Skye asks as she pulls herself closer to me.

'Maybe.' Thoughts of Cole coming to Frankie's to seek his revenge run freely in my mind. In the past I would never have thought he'd be capable of doing something like this, but after today I no longer know what anyone is capable of. My judgement is seriously lacking and I need to work on that asap.

'Nah... there's no way Cole would have done something like this.' Bennett says as he leans down to take a closer look. 'Jett warned him off you after the game and he'd be a fool to come straight here and do this to you. It would be like signing his own death warrant.'

'Great. But that doesn't get me home any faster does it.'

'You could always crash at mine.'

I look at Skye and offer her a small smile of thanks. 'I would, but like I said, I have classes super early and I need to make sure I'm on campus so I can get to them.'

'Don't sweat it. I'm heading back that way now if you want a ride?' Bennett says, pushing himself up after analyzing the damage.

'On one condition...'

'Shoot...'

'I don't want to hear Jett's name come out of your mouth once.'

He laughs back at me and says, 'You got it.'

CHAPTER TWENTY-NINE
JETT

I look at the clock and pace the living area again.

It's almost one in the morning and Mila hasn't arrived back yet. Is she trying to make me have a heart attack? I was so close to driving out to Coldwater to check on her when Sienna held me back and told me to give her some space. It probably wasn't the right thing to do to actually listen to my little sister, because now I've been waiting for her to walk through that door for hours.

What if something has happened to her?

What if Cole decided to go pay her a visit. Nah… I don't need to worry about that waste of spunk. Now that Mila has had a taste of me, there's no way in hell she'd be tempted to go back to him. No fucking way. Another wild thought enters my mind… what if some of these desperate puck bunnies have decided to follow her to work… to warn her away from me. I shake my head, easily removing that thought.

Mila is strong-willed and strong headed. She doesn't listen to anything I have to say so there's no way she's going to listen to a bunch of chicks. No. Mila is more than capable of holding her own.

So, where the fuck is she then?

I'm just about to reach for my keys and head out when the front door opens, and I find Mila dripping from head to toe. 'Where the fuck have you been?' I demand, a little on the harsh side. She doesn't answer me. Instead, she just glares at me, her face blank and her hazel eyes void of any kind of emotion.

Her small body moves closer, and she looks at me once more before she tries to move past me. I don't think so. No way is she about to walk away from me. I reach out automatically, blocking her path, forcing her to look at me. 'I'm talking to you.' I try to keep my voice calm and steady but it leaves my lips on a heated whisper.

'What do you want?' She hurls back at me. 'Don't you think you've humiliated me enough for one day?'

I search her face, desperately trying to get some kind of read on her but she's closed off, like a book. 'Humiliate you? What do you mean?' Now she has my head in a spin. I thought things were going great before the game and now it's like she's come back with someone else's personality. Talk about fucking whiplash.

'Are you being serious. Wait... did you think that I wouldn't find out about your stupid little game?'

'We won... but you already know that because you were there.'

'I'm not talking about the fucking hockey game.' She growls back at me and she's fast losing what patience she has left. 'You made me wear your jersey for your own gain. You didn't ask me to wear it because you wanted me to. No, you asked me so you could get one over on Cole.' Her eyes burn into mine, her chest rising and falling at a rapid rate and I can tell she's upset. 'You used me...'

I hang my head in defeat. I know how this looks. Hell, I know how this sounds, but that was never my intention. Well, not all of my intentions anyway. Yes, I wanted to get one over on Cole, he's had it coming to him for years, but I also wanted Mila at the game, letting the whole of Greenmount know that she was mine... and I thought maybe I could be hers. But as usual, it sure looks like I've gone and fucked that up too.

Running a weary hand through my hair, I shake my head and admit it out loud. 'Yeah, I did. There's no point in lying. I used you to get to Cole and I'm not going to apologize for it. I wanted to show that jerk that you don't need him anymore. I wanted him to see that you were too fucking good for him. Is that so bad?'

Mila shakes her head, a look of defeat etched onto her small, delicate heart-shaped face. Did she want me to lie to her? If she'd asked me a few days ago then I would have been able to lie to her face, no fucking problem... but now, when I look at her the truth flows out of me freely... effortlessly. 'And what... am I supposed to need you? Am I supposed to be thankful to you for trying to get one over on my ex?'

'I'd like you to need me.' I whisper before I have a chance to stop myself. I move closer toward her and I breathe a sigh of relief when she doesn't back away. 'I want you to need me the way I need you, Mila. You might think that I'm playing games and believe me, no one is more shocked than me, but I'm done playing games. I wanted you in my shirt to prove a point, I'll admit it. But I also wanted you in my shirt so the whole world could see that you're mine... and I'm yours if you will have me.'

All I can hear is the loud tick of my clock with each passing second.

Mila didn't buy my deep and personal. I don't blame her, but as with most things, me getting into a deep and meaningful was another first for me and I don't think she could appreciate or understand just how hard that was for me to do. Sure, she listened to me pour my heart out and as soon as I'd finished, she didn't say a fucking word. Not a single one. Instead, she decided to take one last look at me and walk away.

I didn't even have the energy to stop her and now she's fast asleep in her room and I'm all alone in mine.

This is not how tonight should have ended up. This is not the way I'd planned for things to go.

At least that's what I intended, but the pull toward Mila was too strong. I needed to set things right with her. I needed to be close to her. I lasted about ten minutes before I made my way to her room, and I'd decided I wasn't going anywhere until she listened to what I had to say.

CHAPTER THIRTY
MILA

'This is getting quite the habit.' Jett whispers against my neck and all the small hairs stand to attention. 'If we're not careful people are going to start talking.'

A small laugh escapes me as I slowly roll over onto my side so I can get a better look at him. 'People are talking already, or didn't you pay attention yesterday?' I ask and his eyes glitter with danger. I like watching Jett when he's like this. So calm and carefree, and I like to think that I'm the only person who gets to see this real side to him.

'Oh, I was paying attention alright, but only to you.'

'Yeah... I bet you say that to all the girls.' I laugh again, but on the inside, I can't help but feel a little self-conscious. How am I supposed to trust Jett now after everything that happened yesterday. I'm weak when I'm around him. I have zero self-control. Last night he poured his heart out to me, and we made up, but that doesn't mean everything he says to me is the truth.

He's a master manipulator and I'm the willing victim who falls hook, line, and sinker every single time. I promised myself I'd be stronger around him, yet here I am lay next to him once again, butt naked like I don't have any self-respect.

He moves his head, nuzzling his mouth into my neck and my whole body turns to liquid butter under his touch. I have no way of thinking straight when he's this close to me. My mind is clouded, pulled into a Jett induced coma. Sure, it's a nice place to be, but not when I have things to think on and classes to attend.

'I don't understand you at all.' I confess.

'So, let's not complicate things.' He laughs back. 'This feels good. It feels right so how about we just roll with it instead of over thinking things?'

He won't find me arguing with him on that front. Without another thought, Jett rolls on top of me, pinning me beneath him and right in this moment I don't think I can think of any other place I'd rather be.

I'm happy here. Secluded in our little bubble. The chaos of the outside world instantly forgotten, if only for a short while.

I climb out of the shower and the smell of cooked bacon invades my senses. I dress quickly, throwing on a pair of skinny jeans, a light blue tea and a long cardigan and head downstairs.

I find Jett in the kitchen, singing away to himself as he cooks up a storm. What is this parallel universe that I've stepped into. I sure as hell didn't have Jett down as the type of guy who liked to cook and get loose in the kitchen, yet here we are. I'm about to take a seat at the kitchen table when a knock sounds at the door. I glance at the clock and see it's still early, but don't think much of it.

'I'll grab it.' I call over my shoulder to Jett and he offers me a small murmur in response. Maybe it's Bennett coming to check in to see how the land lies after last night, or maybe it could be one of Jett's many admirers. I open the door and don't recognize the lady standing in front of me, but she looks very formal.

'Miss Daniels?'

I bite down on my lips as I take in her smart attire. No one should be knocking on this door for me. Especially someone looking as smart as this woman. 'Who's asking?' I ask, a little on the defensive.

'Miss Daniels, my name is Mrs. Blunt. I'm The Dean's personal secretary. He's asked if you could accompany me to his office.' Her voice is small and a flash of pity dances in her eyes. My heart stops and sinks to my chest.

I know what this is about. My worst nightmare is about to come true. The clerical office obviously made a massive mistake when they offered me a place and now that I'm settled in, the error must have flagged up on the system and now they're going to kick me out of Greenmount.

'Who is it?' Jett calls over my shoulder as he makes his way to the door. 'Oh, Miss Blunt, can I help you with anything?' He asks, curiosity lacing his tone.

'Mr. Jameson, the Dean has asked that Miss Daniels' come to his office immediately.' Her voice is clipped, and you can tell she's the one who's been handed the short stick. You can tell just by looking at her scrunched up face she'd rather be anywhere than here delivering my life changing news.

'Can't you tell me what this is about... in private?' I plead, feeling a rush of heat sweeping into my cheeks.

She shakes her head, and the flash of pity is there again. 'Miss Daniels, the Dean needs to see you.' She looks over my shoulder at Jett. 'It's probably best you come too, Mr. Jameson. It's a matter of urgency.'

CHAPTER THIRTY-ONE
MILA

It felt like an absolute lifetime walking up to the main building.

No matter how far I walked, the main building didn't seem to be getting any closer. Everything around me feels off and I can't believe this is actually happening to me. Hidden deep in the back of my mind I knew this would happen. Being offered a place at the prestigious Greenmount sure sounded too good to be true, and now it looks like I was right all along.

I just wish they would have picked up on the error before I'd actually rocked up here with my six boxes of minimal belongings. It sure would have saved me heaps of embarrassment.

The air thickens as the silence brews between us. Miss Blunt hasn't said more than two words since we left the apartment and her whole aura is off. Pity is oozing out of her every pore, which only makes me feel worse. Surely, she could have told me back at the apartment and I would have been able to pack up and drive out of campus without anyone else witnessing my epic downfall. And to make matters worse this is all happening with Jett beside me.

I feel the heat of his eyes burning into me. I refuse to look at him. If I act like he isn't here, then maybe I'll be able to force it into my reality and he'll disappear.

'Are you okay?' He whispers as he brings his large frame closer to mine, the heat from his body instantly consumes me and it takes everything I have to keep my eyes focused straight ahead, at the big building—the building where my dreams have come to die.

His elbow gently nudges me as he tries to get my attention. I want to scream and shout, desperate to know why this is happening to me, but I know that if I allow an ounce of emotion to escape me then I'll crumble on the spot. It's hard enough trying to keep my emotions in check and I know, one wrong move and it will be game over.

'Hey... what's with the silent treatment.' He presses but thankfully I'm saved from answering him when Miss Blunt turns back toward me when we reach the marble steps of the main office.

'Miss Daniels, if you'd please follow me. The Dean is waiting for you.'

An icy shudder runs down my spine when her brown eyes meet mine, and she looks at me like she wants to reach out and comfort me, to tell me this is all going to be okay. I wish I could believe her, but how the hell is this going to be okay? I'm going to be sent packing, on my merry way back to Coldwater. Personally, I can't think of a worse fate.

'You've got this.' Jett whispers into my ear and I shake my head in defeat. Silently begging him to leave me alone. But then this is the elusive Jett Jameson we're talking about. He's relentless. He doesn't stop, period.

As if my current predicament isn't bad enough, not content with the despair they've caused me already, the Dean doesn't see me straight away. Miss Blunt silently walked me and Jett through the glass entrance, nothing but the sound of her killer heels clicking against the stone slabs as we made our way to my demise.

'Any idea what this is about?' Jett asks, finally breaking the stagnant silence between us and I narrow my eyes at him.

'What do you think?' I hurl back, the venom heavy on my tongue. I know I'm taking all my anger out on him, but what else am I supposed to do? I haven't said a word since we left so surely, he can tell I don't want to talk about it. 'I'm in the dark just as much as you.'

He holds his hands up in surrender and I instantly feel bad for being a bitch. That wasn't my intention, but I can't help it. My whole body is on pins right now. My heart is pounding deep inside my chest and my stomach is in knots. 'I'm sorry. I'm just trying to help, is all.' His voice is small and soft, which only makes me feel ten times worse.

'Miss Daniels...' Miss Blunt's head appears behind the Dean's office, and I raise my eyes reluctantly. 'Dean O'Donoghue will see you now. Please, come in.'

This is it. This is game over for me, I just know it. Why else would I be called to the Dean's office without any further explanation. I reluctantly push myself up, my palms cold and clammy as the fear kicks in. I look behind me and find that Jett is hot on my heels. I guess my bitchy attitude hasn't scared him off then.

I step inside the dimly lit office and find an athletic man with hazel eyes watching me. He smiles at me, but the smile doesn't reach his eyes. 'Mila...' he says. 'May I call you Mila?' I nod back at him, unable to find the words to respond to him in a respectful manner. To be fair if he's about to send me packing from Greenmount then he won't find a trace of respect in me for him and his place here.

He nods at Jett in acknowledgement, clear that they know each other. 'Please take a seat.'

I swallow down on the hard lump which has formed at the back of my throat. 'I'd like to stay standing.' Whatever he has to say to me then he can say it now. I'd much rather get this humiliation over and done with. The sooner the words have left his lips, the sooner I can turn around and walk out of here with my head held high, before anyone can figure out what's really happened.

'As you wish...' he nods before placing his elbows on the table and bringing his hands together. He looks between me and Jett while he tries to figure out the best way to deliver the dream shattering news. 'I don't know how to tell you this...'

'Please... whatever it is, please tell me.' I say breathlessly, unable to take more of the torturous unknown.

'Are you sure you wouldn't like to take a seat?'

Shit... this is bad. It has to be worse than I feared if he's making sure I'm seated comfortably before he delivers the lethal blow. But what could be worse than getting kicked out? 'I'm good standing, sir.' I burn my eyes into his, pleading with him to hurry up and get this over with.

'Okay... well, there's no easy way to say this, Mila. I'm afraid there has been an accident...'

An accident? I haven't been in an accident. 'What do you mean? I'm not following?' Confusion creeps onto my face as I try and fail to figure out where he's going with this. I sense Jett coming closer to me and the whole atmosphere in the Dean's office changes. Like they know something serious... something I'm yet to discover.

'Your mom has been found unconscious.' The Dean looks between me and Jett, deciding how best to break the news. Quickly deciding what he should and shouldn't disclose. 'Your mother is being blue lighted to Coldwater Medical as we speak, but I'm afraid we've been told she's critical and to expect the worst.'

'What... what happened?' I stammer, struggling to process the words. This can't be right. He must have the wrong person. If something was wrong with my mom, then someone would have called me. They would have told me sooner.

Silence fills the small room and I feel like the walls are caving in on me. My chest tightens, constricting and preventing the correct airflow to circulate from my mouth to my lungs. 'All we know so far is that it's a suspected overdose.'

I fall down into the seat, my body giving up under the weight of the pressure. 'I can't get there.' I look around the room, desperate for someone to help me. Jett doesn't take his eyes away from me and for the first time I see pure emotion looking back at me. 'Someone slashed my tire last night. I don't have a ride...' I mutter more to myself, my mind on overdrive as I try to figure out how I'm going to get to my mom's side.

'I'll take you.' Jett drops down by my side so he can talk to me at eye level. 'Don't worry about getting there. I've got you covered.' He leans in and whispers in my ear, 'I'm here, princess. Whatever you need, I'll make sure you have it. I won't let you down.'

My heart goes wild in my chest, and I struggle to regulate my breathing.

I can see everyone around me, but it feels like I'm on the outside looking in and there's nothing I can do to stop this nightmare from unfolding right before my very eyes. The Dean's words sound out around in my head, stuck on repeat like a broken fucking record.

'Suspected overdose...'

What the hell? It doesn't even make sense. Sure, everyone knows my mom is an alcoholic. There's no secrets there, and she probably enjoyed a whole heap of other illegal shit when Dan was on the scene, but my mom knew her limits. She wasn't stupid enough to take more than her body could handle. She knew what she could take. She fucking knew what her body could handle, and I know for a fact my mom wouldn't have taken a deliberate overdose. She's as stubborn as they come and there's no way she'd want to end it all.

CHAPTER THIRTY-TWO
JETT

Mila looks broken. Completely damaged beyond repair.

I've never seen her look so small, and it breaks my icy heart knowing there's not much I can do for her right now.

Mila has never openly spoken about her life outside of Greenmount. She sure as hell never mentioned her mom, but then why should she? If Mila is anything like me, then she's probably used this experience to get away from the demons of her past.

It's in this painful moment, as she hangs her head in pain that I realize the two of us are more alike than I ever thought possible.

I stand, reluctantly giving Mila a little breathing space. I don't want to go anywhere. I want to pull her into the safety of my arms and protect her from the inevitable pain which is about to come crashing into her life.

I can't change things, but I'll make sure that I'm the one who's by her side. Mila doesn't trust me all too much and for good reason, but this is my chance to prove to her that underneath the hardened exterior I can be the good guy. I might just convince myself in the process that I actually have feelings instead of shutting them off all the goddamn time.

Reaching out, I place my hand protectively on her shoulder to let her know that I'm here. I'm here and I'm not leaving her side, not even for a nano-second. She flinches under my heated touch, but she doesn't push me away, so that has to count for something.

'I'll take her to the hospital.' I confirm out loud, on the off chance that they didn't hear me the first time. 'Come on.' My hand slides down her back, offering her support and encouraging her to stand. I need to snap her back to the here and now before she succumbs to the shock. I'm surprised when she doesn't resist and stands. She takes one last look at the Dean and Miss Blunt before walking straight out of the door. Her head is down and I can tell she's already starting to close off to the outside world.

She doesn't say anything until we arrive back the apartment. She stops at the door before turning to face me. 'I don't need your help.' She bites out, her eyes glistening with unshed tears which are threatening to spill over. 'I can make my own way.'

'Mila, you don't have a ride.' I move toward her, but she moves backwards, like she can't seem to put enough space between us.

'I'll call an Uber.' She deadpans, and there is zero emotion in her voice.

'Like fuck you will.' I shout back, fast losing my patience. This is not her fault but I need her to snap out of her miss independent routine and allow me to take her back to Coldwater. Didn't she hear what the Dean said?

Her mom is critical.

That means any second now she could die, and Mila is standing here, prepared to wait around for a ride when she has me and my car at her disposal. 'I'm taking you and that's final.' My voice is more authoritative this time. I'm uncomfortable in the knowledge that she's hurting and there's nothing I can do to make this better for her. If I could swap places with her, I'd do it in a heartbeat, but I'm wise enough to keep that thought to myself.

Without a moment's hesitation, I close the distance between her and grab her hand, holding it protectively in mine. 'Allow me to do this for you, princess. We need to get to the medical center as soon as possible. When we get there if you want me to leave then I'll go, I promise. Just please let me get you there in one piece.'

This time I'm thankful she doesn't argue with me. Instead, she nods and climbs into my car. I don't know what we'll find when we get there, but I'll make sure I'm by her side every step of the way, even if it's from a distance.

No one should have to experience losing a mom, and if they do then they sure as hell shouldn't experience it alone. I'm a walking, talking testament to that. Losing a parent fucks you up like nothing else, and I swear I won't allow the same fate to happen to Mila. I know what it's like to be left out in the dark, regardless of whether it was for my best interests, but Mila isn't cut out for a lifetime of those demons.

CHAPTER THIRTY-THREE
MILA

Jett rolls over the engine of his black jeep commander as I keep my wet eyes focused out the window, desperately trying to wrap my head around this mess. I can't believe I thought I was about to be kicked out of Greenmount, when all along my mom was lying face down in the apartment somewhere unconscious. Obviously, I'm just as self-centered as she's always been. The apple doesn't fall far from the tree, as they say.

'Do you want to talk about it?' Jett asks as we hit Coldwater's intersection, breaking the heavy silence which has blanketed us so far on the drive. The atmosphere changes, dropping to an icy temperature to reflect my current mood.

I don't say anything but I snap my eyes toward him and see a mixture of pity and concern looking back at me. Another solid lump of uncontrollable emotion forms deep in my throat, and all I manage is a small shake of my head. The truth is I don't want to talk about it. I don't even want to think about it.

Guilt ripples through me and crushes my chest when I think about how I could have done more. Would this have happened if I'd checked in on her more.

What if she was calling me last night as a cry for help? What if my mom needed me and I was too busy thinking of myself. What kind of person does that make me if I'm happy to put myself before the needs of others.

The smell of bleach hits me as soon as we walk into the medical center, burning my nostrils as we walk through the main entrance. All of my senses are on high alert, aware at any moment someone could come rushing toward me telling me that my mom didn't make it.

I breathe in deep as I approach the desk and a small plump brown-haired lady greets me. Her smile is too pleasant to be in an emergency room, but I decide against commenting on it. I have to remember that my pain is real right now and she just works here. She doesn't have any personal connection to my mom, so why wouldn't she be friendly?

'How can I help?' She asks, looking between me and Jett as he stands by my side, like my own personal bodyguard. I'm sure one day I'll be grateful for his support, but right now all I can focus on is finding my mom.

'I'm looking for Natalie Daniels.' I stammer... 'She was brought in with the ambulance. Suspected overdose.' The words don't even sound right as I say them. They sound wrong. So, fucking wrong.

She looks at her computer, clicking on her keyboard a couple of times as she searches for my mom and it feels like a lifetime. Maybe this has all been one big understanding and it isn't even my mom who has been brought in. All too soon the lady looks up at me and tells me to head straight down to the end of the corridor and I'd find my mom in Intensive care.

Everything stops and I take in her words and if Jett wasn't stood behind me, I'm pretty sure I would have fallen straight to the floor as my body crumples beneath me. 'I've got you, princess.' He whispers in my ear as he wraps a strong arm around my waist, holding me up, making sure I don't fall just like he promised. He takes my hand, squeezing it tight so I have no choice of letting go as he takes the lead. When I look at him, I see his jaw is set and the vein at his temple is throbbing violently.

'Are you okay?' I ask, suddenly feeling like he's starting to feel more uncomfortable than me. I don't think I've ever witnessed him looking so green.

'Hospitals aren't my thing.' He replies. 'But this isn't about me, princess.'

I stop walking hoping to put off the inevitable for as long as possible and decide to use Jett as the reason. 'If you don't want to be here you can leave.' My eyes search his, trying to get a better read on him. I'm grateful he's here but I don't want him to make himself feel uncomfortable for my benefit. I can deal with this with or without him. She's my mom, not his.

He moves closer to me, his minty breath tickling my face as he cups my chin, forcing me to look at him. 'I'm here. I'm not going anywhere, so quit worrying about me and focus on your mom.' He warns and I know better than to argue back with him. Instead, I offer him a small nod and allow him to lead the rest of the way.

I don't think anyone could have prepared me for what I was about to walk into.

I found my mom's room and I barely recognized her. Her face, of what I could see of it was pale, lifeless, and tubes and machinery were covering most of her body. This isn't my mom. Not how I knew her. My mom is a shell of her former self and I instantly hate myself for ignoring her.

I could have saved her. I could have stopped this from happening if only I'd given her a few minutes of my time.

If anything happens to her, I don't think I'll ever forgive myself.

'Miss Daniels...' an unfamiliar voice calls out from behind me and when I turn, I see a tall slim man with a receding hairline in a doctors jacket looking right at me. 'If you'd like to come this way.'

I look at Jett, unsure what to do and when he nods back at me encouragingly, I know I need to follow the doctor. I force myself to put one unsteady foot in front of the other. He leads us to the family room and I've watched enough drama's to know that the family room is where they deliver the bad news.

'You don't need to come in with me.'

Jett holds my hand tighter, keeping me close to his side, holding on like he's never going to let go and I'm not about to complain. 'Seriously. Do you really think I'm about to let you go through this alone?' He breathes and his eyes are ablaze with emotion. 'I'm here and I'm not going anywhere.

'Thanks, but I'm a big girl.'

'I don't doubt it,' a small smile curves his lips as he says. 'But I meant what I said, princess. You're my girl, and there's no way I'm going to let you go through this alone.'

I walk into the room and take a seat opposite the doctor. His face is unreadable, but then I guess it has to be in this kind of profession. 'How is she?' I ask, not sure if I'm ready to hear the answer.

'Stable, for now.' He looks at me over his glasses. 'Your mom is currently in a critical condition and the next twenty-four hours will be hit and miss. She was found unconscious and as she was alone, we have no idea how long she was in that medical state. We administered naloxone, a drug to reverse the damage and effects of any opioid drugs she may have taken...'

'Drugs?' I exclaim. This has Dan written all over it, and what the hell was she doing alone? Did he leave her for dead?

'We're still waiting for blood work to come back, but when it's a suspected overdose, we use the reversal medication so we don't leave anything out. Unfortunately, your mom then went into cardiac arrest and experienced some down time. We decided to put her into an induced coma to aid any chance of recovery, no matter how small.'

'None of this is making any sense.' I bite down on my lower lip, worrying it between my teeth as I try to process everything the doctor is saying to me, but all I hear is white noise.

'I appreciate this is overwhelming for you, but I can assure you your mom is in the best hands and we will do everything we can for her. I have to let you know that because of her downtime she experienced some lack of oxygen before we regained a steady pulse, and we won't know the extent of damage until she regains consciousness.'

'What kind of damage are we talking, doc?' Jett asks when he realizes I've lost the functionality of speaking.

'When the heart stops, the brain doesn't receive oxygen and after as little as four minutes the brain cells begin to die...' he looks at me to check I'm taking in what he's saying. 'We don't know what damage has been done until she's conscious, but we have a brain scan booked tomorrow for any potential signs of brain damage.' He leans across the table. 'I know this is a lot to take in, but first we need to get your mom through the next twenty-four hours.'

I feel like I've awoken into one of my worst nightmares. None of this sounds real. It can't be real.

Before I have a chance to say anything else, his pager sounds and he stands. 'I'm sorry. I need to go...' he rushes to the door, and alarms fill the hall before he rushes straight into my mom's room, and I instantly fear the worst.

The last thing I remember is Jett reaching out to catch me as I went to stand, and the world went black. I didn't fight it. I had no energy left in me to fight, and I willingly gave myself up, succumbing to the darkness.

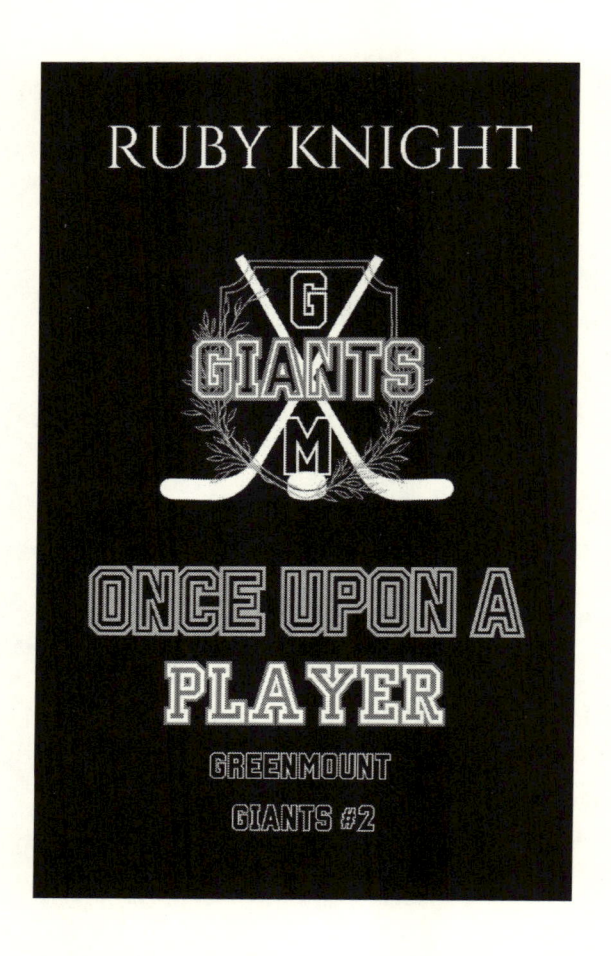

PRE-ORDER THE NEXT INSTALMENT NOW

www.books2read.com/onceuponaplayer

A NOTE FROM THE AUTHOR

Thank you so much for picking up a copy of

ONCE UPON A ROOMMATE

I hope you enjoy the beginning of Jett and Mila's story.

Come join us in [Ruby Knight's Dark Romancers](#)

Made in the USA
Columbia, SC
29 February 2024